of DooM

CIRCLE
of DOOM

Tim Kennemore

Andersen Press • London

For Tom and Ruth

First published in 2001 by
Andersen Press Limited,
20 Vauxhall Bridge Road, London SW1V 2SA
www.andersenpress.co.uk

Reprinted 2002

British Library Cataloguing in Publication Data available
ISBN 1 84270 044 8

The   Islands

Contents

1

Hocus Pocus

The Sharp family had lived at Cleve Cottage for so long that even Lizzie, who was the oldest of the children and who had been three when they moved there, could remember no other home. Cleve Cottage was at the very farthest end of Cleve Road, which was the very last road in the village, and apart from The Briars, which was directly opposite, and didn't count, the nearest house was a fifteen-minute walk away, and you had go three times that far to get to houses where other children lived.

The Briars didn't count because nobody young lived there and nobody ever visited. It was the home of a very, very old couple called Mr and Mrs Potward, who kept themselves to themselves, and were generally unhelpful and irritated about perfectly reasonable things. If a ball landed in their garden they might not let you have it back till next week, to teach you a lesson. They were the sort of people who turned the lights off and pretended to be out if they heard carol singers approaching, and cheerful noise of any kind caused them great agitation. They were mean-spirited and cross, and the house was much too big for them, and there was nothing left in the world that gave them any pleasure, and it was the opinion of the Sharp children (though they did not say so in front of their parents) that they really might as well be dead.

And of course the worst of it was that as long as the Potwards lived at The Briars there was not the slightest chance of a proper family with children moving in.

On Lizzie's thirteenth birthday the Potwards ruined her party and she decided to become a witch and magic them to destruction. It was a garden party, and the sun shone and it would have been perfect. But after only half an hour the Potwards arrived at her front door to complain about the noise, which was mostly the sound of children enjoying themselves, a thing they found particularly distressing.

'It brings on Stanley's arthritis,' said Mrs Potward. 'I should have thought you might show some consideration.'

'Young people nowadays haven't got any consideration,' said Mr Potward, all shrivelled and grey and grumpy.

'And me at my age, with my hips!'

'And her nerves!'

The Sharp children looked at their parents without much hope. They all knew perfectly well that noise didn't make hips or arthritis worse and that there was nothing wrong with the Potwards except bad temper, most of which was caused by living longer than they rightfully should. But:

'We'll move the party indoors, Mrs Potward,' said their father, who believed in keeping on the right side of their neighbours. He also believed that you should never let the sun go down on your anger, that you all had to live together so you might as well try to get along, and that there was good in everybody. His children thought he was soft.

The party had to be moved. It was the last straw.

'I'm going to make a magic potion,' said Lizzie the next day. 'I am going to cast a spell upon the Grotwards. I have had *enough*.'

'There's no such thing as magic,' said Dan, who was ten, and sensible.

Max was only seven, and was not completely sure yet about magic. There were so many puzzling things in the world. He had only just worked out answerphones, and still couldn't understand fax machines, which seemed excellent evidence that magic was everywhere.

'Well, I'm going to try,' said Lizzie, who had a mass of dark hair, and a longer nose than she would have liked, and who did indeed look quite witchy at times. She went into the kitchen and assembled her ingredients. First she picked out a rather mouldy-looking apple and orange from the fruitbowl, and a small tomato from the vegetable rack. She chopped them up and threw them into the Sharps' largest stewpot, which made a wonderful cauldron, added a pint of water and turned it up to boil. Her brothers watched in silence. Max's mouth was gaping wide open with amazement; Dan was shaking his head at the madness of it all.

'Four of the magic ingredients are already boiling!' said Lizzie. 'Only two remain.'

'Can I fetch one?' asked Max. 'Please?'

Lizzie thought for a few moments and said: 'Pepper!'

Max handed Lizzie the pepper mill and climbed up on

3

a stool so he could see into the pot.

'Ten turns!' said Lizzie, grinding the mill. A cloud of black pepper drifted down into the cauldron. Lizzie sneezed, three times in a row.

Pepper, thought Dan. An orange and an apple. A tomato. Was there any meaning to it? Lizzie might be mad but she was generally mad in a logical sort of way, whereas most girls he knew were just mad, full stop. Why had she not used the mushrooms, which looked just the thing to boil up in a potion? Or that nasty shrivelled courgette? There must be a pattern. One thing was for sure: he wasn't having anything to do with it. 'And so, what's the last thing going to be then?' he asked. 'Shredded batwing? Toad's toenails? Frog warts? Powdered spider?'

'The last ingredient is indeed the most difficult,' said Lizzie, stirring vigorously.

'I'll get it for you, Lizzie,' said Max. He had never been a witch's assistant before, and he was starting to think it was the most exciting thing that had ever happened to him since they'd let him be goalkeeper in the playground football game the day Nathan Dursley was away.

Lizzie gave him a long look.

'The fetching of the last ingredient is a very special task,' she said, in a ghostly sort of whisper. 'You must not fail.'

'Tell me!' begged Max. He wanted to do this more than anything in the world, especially as it couldn't possibly involve letting in twenty-three goals and being called a useless bogslime.

Lizzie bent down and whispered in his ear. His eyes widened.

'Are you sure?'

'Positive!' said Lizzie. 'Take a piece of enchanted binding cloth!'

'Looks like kitchen roll to me,' said Dan, but they ignored him. Max scampered off into the garden, returning a few minutes later with something carefully folded inside the enchanted binding cloth. Lizzie was sneezing again. Dan wrinkled his nose. The magic potion was beginning to smell rather nasty, and the adding of the final ingredient made it a good deal worse.

'Wash your hands!' Lizzie told Max. Max scuttled towards the sink and started scrubbing. 'And then, fetch me the magic potion vial!'

'Wossthat?' said Max.

Lizzie pointed towards the back door.

'Looks like an empty milk bottle to me,' said Dan. Lizzie turned off the cooker, rummaged in the cupboards till she found a plastic funnel, and carefully poured her potion into the vial. 'There!' she said.

The potion looked absolutely disgusting. It was a pinky-brown colour, with clods of tomato and orange mush floating and disintegrating in the most unpleasant way. It looked like what would happen in your stomach just before you were sick.

'It's brilliant!' said Max, gazing with admiration.

'If you go and drink that you needn't expect me to call the ambulance,' said Dan, although they all knew he would.

Max gulped, and turned rather pale. He hadn't yet thought about what Lizzie was going to do with the potion when it was made. Was she going to drink it? Surely she wasn't going to ask *him* to drink it? He didn't want to let her down, especially not when she was letting him be her assistant, but he knew what the secret ingredient was and he thought quite honestly that if he had to drink any he would probably die.

'Of course I'm not going to drink it,' said Lizzie scornfully. 'We are going to sprinkle it. It must be sprinkled to the North, the South, the East and the West, completing a Circle of Doom.'

'You're making this up as you go along,' said Dan.

Lizzie marched out through the back door, and round the side of Cleve Cottage to the front, where she dodged down behind the hedge and peeked through the edge of the gate at The Briars opposite. Max arrived by her side and squinted through the hedge. Dan strolled across some way behind, whistling. You had to keep an eye on lunatics, for their own good.

'All clear?' asked Lizzie.

'All clear!' whispered Max.

'Follow me,' said Lizzie. She opened the gate, ran across the lane, leapt over the low stone wall at the front of The Briars and dived for cover in the long grass at the side. Max scrambled after her, shaking with excitement and terror. They were *in the Potwards' garden*. What if the Potwards were to come out and catch them? What if old Mrs Potward was looking out of her window this very minute? There would be tremendous trouble. It was worse than anything he had ever done, and more scary and more deliciously exciting.

Lizzie seemed to read his thoughts.

'If anybody sees us, we're looking for specimens!' she hissed. She had no clear idea of what specimens were, but in books when you spotted suspicious characters hiding behind hedges or squatting in shrubberies, they were more often than not perfectly innocent people looking for specimens.

Max squeaked.

'Hocus pocus, double bubble,' said Lizzie mysteriously, and they set off, wriggling through the grass on their stomachs round the very edges of the Potwards' garden, Lizzie sprinkling potion all about.

Dan watched from the safety of the lane that separated their house from The Briars. So many things to worry about all at once. Not only might the Potwards appear, but his parents would be back from the village at any moment. He had to be on the alert. If either of these things happened he would say they had seen a hedgehog with a broken leg. Lizzie and Max had gone to try and find it and save it. He would also have to be ready with first aid in case of damage to his brother and sister. It would probably be poisoning (administer a salt water solution until patient is sick), but it was quite possible that the Potwards kept animal traps in their shrubbery, in which case you were looking at severe blood loss, mangled flesh and possible amputation.

It seemed as if hours passed before Lizzie and Max appeared at the other side of The Briars, along by Potters

Field. They raced down the last stretch and clambered over the wall. Max's cheeks were bright pink and his knees cut and scratched. He looked blissfully happy. He looked like a goalie who has had a hard match but kept a clean sheet.

'Hocus pocus!' said Lizzie, collapsing in a heap on the ground.

'You'll want to get inside and clean that stewpot before Mum and Dad get back,' said Dan, changing back from being anxious to being irritated as soon as he saw they were safe.

'What's this then?' said a voice from inside the Potwards' garden.

It was Mr Potward.

The children froze. Lizzie's heart was pounding like a hammer. Now what could they do?

Mr Potward approached the wall, with a pair of pruning shears in his hand and a look of pure hatred on his face.

Lizzie blurted something about specimens.

Dan blurted something about hedgehogs.

Max squeaked.

Lizzie scrambled to her feet.

'What's all this?' said Mr Potward, pointing to the empty milk bottle in her hand.

'M-m-milk!' said Lizzie. She would have probably gone on to say 'b-b-bottle!' but: 'For the hedgehog!' said Dan.

'What hedgehog?' said Max. He was getting confused. If Lizzie had gone and turned Mrs Potward into a hedgehog, there was *definitely* going to be trouble.

'Take your noise away back to your own house, before Mrs Potward hears you, her with her hip and all!' said Mr Potward. 'And you don't want to be carrying bottles, that's glass, that, what if that breaks and bits go in our garden? Did you want to see Mrs Potward fall and break her neck on a piece of broken glass? Did you?'

The children said nothing. None of them had ever thought of this particular actual mishap befalling Mrs Potward, but there had been many that were extremely similar.

'Surprised your parents allow such gallivanting,' said Mr Potward, and wandered off to prune his roses in a general moany mumbling.

'He didn't see us!' said Lizzie. 'He didn't! For a moment I thought we were dead meat. But he was just looking like that because that's the way he always looks. Gallivanting!' she added. 'Standing in the lane with a milk bottle, and he calls it gallivanting! I expect when he was young his parents kept him in a cage.'

'*You're* likely to end up in a cage if you don't clean that stewpot,' said Dan, and they trailed back indoors, friends again. All of a sudden Lizzie had completely stopped being a witch and gone back to her proper self. This was a huge relief to Dan, who liked things to be straightforward. He didn't even like to see people dressed up for fancy dress parties. It made him very uneasy.

'Is that *all*?' said Max, looking disappointed. Where was the hedgehog? Had the magic worked? He looked back over his shoulder, in case Mr Potward might even at that moment be disappearing in a puff of smoke.

'We've just made a potion, sprinkled a Circle of Doom and nearly been eaten alive by Mr Grotward,' said Lizzie. 'What more do you want?'

'Talking about that potion,' said Dan.

'What about it?' said Lizzie.

'Why did you choose those things to go in it? Why not mushrooms?'

Lizzie laughed. 'Can't you work it out?'

'I know there's some pattern,' said Dan. 'But I can't see what it is.'

'Orange, apple, tomato,' said Lizzie. 'Pepper. I mightn't have used the pepper, because it always makes me sneeze so much. But we were out of parsnips, and Mum's port costs a fortune.'

Dan thought about this. 'It had to begin with P?'

'P for Potward,' said Lizzie. 'Pepper, orange, tomato, water, apple...'

'P, O, T, W, A!' said Dan. All of a sudden it made sense, of a sort. 'I get it. But what about the R and the D?' They walked across the kitchen towards the sink. The unforgettable smell of potion still lingered in the air.

'They were the secret ingredient,' said Lizzie, and set about scrubbing the stewpot. Dan squirted fresh air spray around the room. He wrinkled his brow, trying to work out what the RD could have been. 'Rubber ducks?' he said. 'Rotten daisies? Rabid dog?'

'Not even close,' said Lizzie.

'Erm . . . Ribena drink,' said Dan, without much hope. 'Roger Dumpling.'

'Roger *Dumpling*?'

Max, who knew the right answer, found this so funny he dissolved into a fit of uncontrollable giggles.

'Raspberry doughnut!' said Dan in desperation. 'Roast duvet!'

'Give up?' said Lizzie.

Dan nodded.

'Rabbit droppings!' said Lizzie.

'Rabbit droppings? You mean Max went out there and . . . out of Poppy's hutch . . . but you can't!'

'Lucky it wasn't last week when Poppy was poorly,' said Lizzie, 'or it would have been rabbit diarrhoea.'

'That is *gross*,' said Dan.

'Roger Dumpling!' howled Max. Lizzie and Dan looked at him. It was important that Max, who was not yet very good at keeping secrets, shouldn't tell their parents anything about the Potward Potion. It was not something you could expect parents to understand, not even theirs. But it seemed that if they were to arrive now, all they would get out of Max was a lot of total nonsense about potions, magic hedgehogs and Roger Dumpling. They wouldn't even *listen*.

And of course, Lizzie had only meant the whole thing as a piece of fun to make her feel better about the Potwards spoiling her party. There was no such thing as magic, and she was going to grow up to be an actress, not a witch.

Except that the very next day Mrs Potward fell and

11

hurt her hip, and was bundled away in an ambulance together with her nerves and her rheumatics and Mr Potward, and they never came back ever again.

2

Mortal Remedies

Three weeks later a FOR SALE sign appeared in the garden of The Briars.

'So they're really really gone?' asked Max, who had somehow never quite believed this. The Potwards were just exactly the sort of people who would sneak back in the middle of the night to give you a nasty surprise and teach you a lesson.

'Really *really* gone,' said Lizzie, happily. Lizzie had hastily revised her career plans as a result of recent events. Witchcraft was definitely the correct option. People were always telling her that actresses were continually out of work, resting between jobs starving and penniless. As a witch however she would be self-employed and independent. She would be a GOOD witch, only ever harming those who truly deserved it. The rest of the time she would make love potions and wealth and health and happiness potions and generally provide people with all the things they wanted to have. She would of course charge them a great deal of money for this, because her spells would be of the very highest quality and she would be famous. A *celebrity* witch. She would have her own TV show called *The Witching Hour*, publish books of easy spells for beginners and market her own line in shiny copper cauldrons. She would open a chain of shops called *Spell Shack* (or *Lizzie's Kitchen*) where people could buy almost any part of a toad's body (fresh or pickled, whole or pulverised), a dozen different varieties of eyeball, and vials clear and transparent in a full range of handy sizes.

Dan gave her a dark look. He was as glad as anybody else that the Potwards had gone, but the timing and nature of their departure had been extremely unfortunate. Anybody with any sense could see that Mrs Potward's accident had been total coincidence. But now both Lizzie and Max believed that Lizzie had magical powers, which was bound to cause a great deal of trouble.

Lizzie was gazing over at The Briars, her nose pressed up against the kitchen window. 'People may start arriving to look at the house at any time!' she said. 'We have to keep it under constant surveillance.'

'What?' asked Max, joining her at the window. 'Is that a magic spell?'

'No,' said Lizzie. 'It means we have to watch out for the people.'

'We have to watch all day long?' It was wonderful that Lizzie still seemed to be including Max in her plans, but this one didn't sound very exciting.

'I'll draw up a surveillance rota,' said Lizzie.

'So, we're just going to leave school, are we?' asked Dan. 'That's fine. I'm sure everyone will understand. It's not as if education is important or anything, not when there are *houses* to be watched.'

Lizzie thought for a moment. 'We could tape a tiny

thread across the front door opening, and it would break if anyone went in. So we'd know if anybody had been in the house while we weren't here.'

'Oh, well, that's useful!' said Dan, with heavy sarcasm.

Lizzie could see that it wasn't, but it sounded fun just the same. If only you could somehow attach one end of the tiny thread to a mechanism which activated a hidden camera, then FLASH! you'd have a photo of the people who opened the door...

'We could ask Dad to watch for us while we're at school,' said Max.

'Dad's office is at the back of the house,' said Dan, 'and he never notices anything while he's working anyway. Three rhinoceroses and a baby elephant could come and look at the Potwards' house and Dad wouldn't notice.'

'Why would rhinoceroses have a baby elephant?' asked Max. 'They wouldn't. They'd have a baby rhinoceros.'

'Baby rhinoceros?' said their father, who had just at that moment arrived in the kitchen in search of coffee. He was a writer, and required a great deal of coffee to keep his thoughts flowing smoothly. 'Forget it. You've got enough pets already.'

The Sharp children did indeed have a great many pets. Apart from their dog Bonnie, who was three-quarters golden retriever (nobody knew about the other quarter), they had three cats, Snowball, Sapphire and Lucy, Poppy the rabbit, and four guinea pigs called Brandy,

Whisky, Cider and Rum. They had two budgerigars, Billy and Lily. Max had a hamster called Zippy, and at the end of the garden, in their own enclosure of high wire netting, were half a dozen chickens, all named Foxfood. This was their mother's idea. She said it was ridiculous giving chickens their own names when nobody could tell them apart, and it was a mistake to get too attached to them, and by far the best thing was to call them all Foxfood so that you were continually reminded of their eventual destiny.

Lizzie's theory was that her parents were so very generous with pets as a kind of compensation for making them live in the back of beyond, deprived of human companions. All three children made the most of it. You only had to say the word 'gerbil' and by teatime three would have arrived; whenever anything died, its tearful owner was always offered an immediate replacement.

'Dad,' said Max. 'You'd notice if there were three rhinoceroses and a baby elephant in the Potwards' house, wouldn't you?'

'I think I might notice that,' said his father. 'This sounds like an old joke. How do you fit four elephants into a car? Two in the back, two in the front. How do you get four rhinoceroses into a car? You can't, it's already full of elephants.' He chuckled. The children gazed at him in silence. 'OK, OK. I didn't say it was a *good* joke.'

Max was starting to feel that he was losing track of the conversation. This happened to him a lot. He tried to steer it back to a point he understood. 'Dad,' he said, 'we need you to help us watch for people arriving to look at the house.'

'No need to watch,' said his father. 'You'll hear, if anybody comes. How many cars ever come down Cleve Road?'

This was true. Because Cleve Road was so far away from everywhere else and didn't lead to anywhere except a field, it was totally quiet and still. Sometimes they didn't see another car for days at a time, and when they did it was usually someone who'd got lost. If people came to look round the Potwards' house the Sharps would hear them coming in plenty of time to mount guard.

Max was secretly relieved not to have to be on a surveillance rota, though he would never ever have let Lizzie know this. All the same, he spent quite a lot of time watching from the kitchen window, wishing with all his heart for something to happen.

Of all the Sharp children, Max was the one who had the worst time of it, living so far away from everything and everybody. Lizzie was already old enough to travel by bus to see her friends, and she was also very very clever at persuading their parents to take her by car. Lizzie's friends seemed to have equally good persuasive powers, since they were often driven over to Cleve Cottage to spend the day, and sometimes the night, with Lizzie. Max was really delighted to see them arrive, but what always happened was that they patted him on the head, said, 'Aww, isn't he *sweet*?' – and disappeared with Lizzie into her room, only ever re-appearing to be fed. This meant Max actually ended up lonelier than ever.

Dan was self-sufficient. He could amuse himself endlessly. He read books; he built and painted model aircraft; he had any number of science kits and always had some complicated project on the go. He was keen on learning carpentry and had a long-term plan to build his own shed in the garden. He had a computer, and spent time on the Internet, which was a sort of magical computer world filled with webs and spiders, and where Max wasn't allowed.

Max was absolutely nothing like this at all, and he suspected he never would be. Max liked doing the kind of things you need other people for. He liked to play tag and hide-and-seek.

He liked to play Alien Invasion, a brilliant game invented by Lizzie which involved dressing up in weird costumes and racing from one secret lunar base to another until Lizzie shouted, 'Invasion!' and you all leapt out at the same time shrieking, 'Surrender!' But Lizzie had tired of this game very quickly, and Dan never liked anything where you had to dress up or disguise yourself, and it was simply not possible to be an invasion all by yourself.

He liked to play Man Utd versus Chelsea, although he wasn't actually much good at football. He was, in fact, totally useless at football. Dan could sometimes be persuaded to start off the game as Chelsea, but what always happened was that he scored twenty-five goals in three minutes and then wandered off to do something by himself, saying that Man Utd needed a lot more practice. And it was totally impossible to continue the game when the entire Chelsea team had left the pitch to go and build a light detector or play on the computer or complete a 3-D jigsaw of a London double-decker bus.

Many children invent imaginary friends to keep them company; Max's situation was so extreme that he had invented an entire imaginary family. They were called the Dumplings. The good thing about having a whole family was that you could get rid of people when you got bored with them and invent new ones. Several Dumplings who had outlived their usefulness had grown up and gone away; new ones were born all the time to replace them. Roger Dumpling, the original, first-ever Dumpling, was still very much present, seeming to be, like Peter Pan, not subject to the normal forces of growing up. Max's other current favourites were called Leela and Hercules. Lizzie said that Hercules Dumpling was the most ridiculous name in the world. It was like calling someone Godzilla Grapefruit or Darth Doughnut, she said. (Max actually thought these were rather good names.) The Dumpling family were not greatly liked by Max's real family; there were so many Dumplings, and nobody except Max ever knew exactly where they were. All too often, you would sit down at an empty chair at the kitchen table only to hear Max yelp with distress because you had just sat on Leela Dumpling and squashed her flat. Unfortunately, Leela (and all the other Dumplings) always seemed to survive this.

19

Roger was the Dumpling who most often kept Max company while he sat watching out of the window for possible buyers of The Briars. And so it was Roger who was the first to hear Max's squeak of excitement when, one afternoon after school, a large silvery-grey car nosed its way down Cleve Road to the very end, and pulled up right outside.

'Lizzie!' shouted Max. 'Lizzie! Dan! Come quick!' Nothing happened, so he raced out into the hall and shouted up the stairs. 'Lizzie! People!'

Lizzie emerged instantly from her bedroom and tumbled down the stairs. Dan followed more slowly behind. Their mother was still out at work and their father had as usual heard nothing at all.

They all took a look out of the kitchen window. The sight they saw was about as bad as it could possibly be.

'Oh *no*,' said Lizzie, wiping her breath off the window pane, as if this might possibly improve the view.

Four adults (two men and two women) had by now got out of the large silvery-grey car. All four of them looked to be at that disagreeable and discontented sort of age where they hadn't quite got old yet but were about to do so very shortly, and had nothing in the world to look forward to except wrinkling, shrivelling and decaying. One of the men and one of the women looked very much alike: tall and bony, with permanently downturned mouths set in faces of that yellowy-brown colour which is brought about by years of smoking and by an excess of vinegar and other sour things in the constitution. The thin man had one foot in plaster and a large pair of metal crutches, with which he swung and hobbled along a few paces behind the rest of them. The other two were fat and pink, and wore heavy shapeless brown coats underneath which they were surely sweating like pigs in the heat of the sunny June afternoon.

All four of them made their way over to The Briars, opened the gate and disappeared inside.

'Well, look at that,' said Dan. 'You see what happens when you interfere with nature?'

Lizzie and Max looked blank.

'You get rid of two horrible grown-ups,' said Dan, 'and a month later, four horrible grown-ups move in. If you get rid of these, probably in another month *eight* horrible grown-ups will move in. In two months from now you'll have sixteen horrible grown-ups. In three months from now you'll have thirty-two. In four months...'

'You have to do something!' said Max, looking hopefully at Lizzie. If ever there was a time for witchcraft, it was now. And he was the witch's special assistant!

'...in six months' time, two hundred and fifty-six horrible grown-ups!' said Dan, darkly.

Across the road, the four horrible grown-ups, after a brief conference in the front garden, had unlocked the front door of the Briars and gone inside.

'I have a plan!' said Lizzie.

'Hocus pocus, double bubble,' breathed Max. Lizzie

21

was going to magic four people into a catastrophic fate. It was, definitely, the best day of his life, apart from the other one.

'Not magic,' said Lizzie. 'You should only use magic when mortal remedies aren't enough. Magic should never be wasted.'

'Mortal remedies?' asked Dan, suspiciously.

Lizzie looked at him thoughtfully. There was no point in giving Dan a task which was too outrageous or he simply wouldn't do it.

'All you have to do,' she told him, 'is to go into the front room, open all the windows and play the violin.'

'But I can't play the violin,' said Dan. He had had three months of lessons once, but the resulting noises had been so screechingly unpleasant, and Dan's progress so painfully slow, that he had given up the struggle (to everyone's considerable relief).

'I know! That's the whole point!' said Lizzie.

Max was close to exploding with excitement. He tugged on Lizzie's arm. 'What do I do? What about me?'

Lizzie bent down, lowered her voice to a whisper and told him.

3

Alcohol and Fits

The sights and sounds that greeted the four horrible grown-ups as they returned to their car were not something they were soon likely to forget.

In the front garden of the house opposite there was a girl, wearing a yellow bikini and a pair of red stiletto-heeled shoes, and dancing. Pop music blared out from a portable radio turned up to full volume. A large golden dog was collapsed by the front door with an alarming-looking puddle of foam seeping out onto the ground around its mouth.

'WE LIKE TO PARTY!' boomed the radio. 'Party time!' shrieked the girl, twirling and gyrating and clapping her hands.

The grown-ups stood stock still and stared.

'What's going on here?' said the thin man with the crutches. 'What's all this dreadful row?'

'Party!' whooped the girl. 'Party on down! We like to party all the time!'

'PARTY PARTY PARTY!' There was another wild whoop, and a very small boy came racing around the side of the house, wearing a lampshade on his head and nothing else at all. The grown-ups looked aghast.

'That boy should cover himself up!' said the fat pink woman.

'We're naturists!' screamed the girl.

The thin woman took a step forward. 'Turn that awful noise off this minute, young lady. I can't hear a word you say!'

The girl waltzed over to the radio and turned the volume down. The noise was instantly replaced by sounds coming from the house of a violin being played quite desperately badly. It sounded like a hundred baby hyenas being tortured, while a vampire committed suicide at the end of the world.

'That's my brother,' said the girl cheerfully. 'He's a prodigy! He has to practise night and day!'

'Prodigy!' spluttered the man on crutches.

'That boy should cover himself up,' said the fat pink woman again.

'The fresh air is so good for his skin diseases,' said the girl, tottering dangerously towards them in her high heels. 'Hello, I'm Lizzie, and we live here! We party all day and we party all night!'

'You what?'

'My dad holds an open air rock festival out there every summer,' said the girl, waving airily towards Potters Field. All four horrible grown-ups turned their heads to the right to look at the field, and then back again to stare at the girl called Lizzie. 'He used to be the drummer with the Black Metal Zombies, until the drugs made his hands shake so badly he couldn't play. And this is my little brother Max!'

'That child should cover himself up,' said the fat woman, more faintly this time. The girl continued blithely with the round of introductions. 'And that's our dog, Deathstar.' All four heads turned once more. 'He's not very well at the moment. He's got mad dog disease. See how he's been foaming at the mouth? But don't worry – you're quite safe as long as he doesn't bite you.'

'Mad dog disease? What's that? He looks like he's half-asleep to me,' said the thin woman.

'That's because of his medication,' said the girl, sadly. 'But at night he goes quite mad. He howls to the moon.'

'WOOW-OOOOO,' howled the small boy.

'So that's us!' said the girl. 'We're just the most fun neighbours in the world! And there's Grandad lives with us as well – he got so lonely after he lost Grandma to alcohol and fits. He's an outpatient at the mental hospital, but he's doing really well! And Dad I've told you about, and Mum – oh my goodness.' The girl's voice suddenly faltered. 'There she is now!' A blue car had been approaching down Cleve Road, its noise totally drowned out by the wailing of the violin. It was now nearly upon them.

'Max!' screeched Lizzie. 'Get inside! It's Mum!' Max wriggled out of the lampshade, dropped it on the ground and streaked indoors just as his mother got out of the car with two carrier bags full of shopping. The heads of the four horrible grown-ups swivelled round to the left to inspect this new development.

'Hello!' said Mrs Sharp cheerfully. 'What in heaven's name is going on here? Some kind of party? Are those my shoes you're wearing without permission, Lizzie?'

Lizzie gulped. There was a general shaking of heads and tutting amongst the four grown-ups.

'I'm so sorry about your poor mother,' said Mrs Sharp. Lizzie blinked, trying in vain to make any sense of this remark. 'Oh, my goodness! And you've had an accident yourself!'

'Fell off a ladder and broke my ankle while I was doing up the exterior paintwork!' said the thin man with the crutches. Lizzie began to realise that her mother's last couple of remarks had not been addressed to her at all. It appeared that her mother knew these people. Surely they could not possibly be friends of hers? Dan and Max tiptoed out of the front door, stepping carefully over the still-dozing Bonnie (alias Deathstar). Max was now wearing a yellow plastic raincoat.

'Oh no!' said Mrs Sharp, still talking to the man with the crutches.

'And would you believe it? It happened the very same day as Mother fell and broke her hip. How's that for coincidence? How's that for an unlucky streak? Eh?'

'No!' said Mrs Sharp.

'Yes!'

'Such dreadful bad luck! I'm *so* sorry, Mr Potward.'

Mr *Potward*? The children exchanged glances of great confusion. It seemed that their mother had gone barking mad. Mr Potward had gone to live in an Old People's Home with his wife. They tiptoed indoors to watch the rest of the scene through the kitchen window. Their mother continued to chatter brightly to the horrible grown-ups for a further five minutes. It wasn't possible to hear the words, but it seemed suddenly all too likely that the grown-up their mother had mistaken for Mr Potward was saying:

'...*alcohol and fits!*'

'...*foaming at the mouth and howling to the moon!*'

'...*party all day and party all night!*'

'...*stark naked but for a lampshade!*'

'Oh jeebers,' said Lizzie, faintly, as her mother swept into the kitchen carrying the two bags of shopping and the lampshade.

'What was this doing in the garden?' asked her mother, brandishing the lampshade. She didn't actually *look* cross. If anything there was the slightest glint of a twinkle in her eyes.

Lizzie and Dan looked at Max.

'I was taking it for a walk!' said Max.

Mrs Sharp put the lampshade down on the kitchen table.

'I see. And Dan. Did I hear the rather surprising sound of you playing my violin, when I got out of the car?'

Max and Lizzie looked at Dan.

'I was cleaning the strings!' said Dan.

'I see. Now, if somebody will just explain to me why the dog is lying in a puddle of Fairy Liquid, I'm sure absolutely everything will start to make sense.'

Dan and Max looked at Lizzie.

'I was washing the garden!' said Lizzie.

'Well,' said their mother, placing the carrier bags on the table by the lampshade, 'it's a great comfort to know that everything is in such capable hands.'

'Of course it is!' said their father, suddenly looming in the kitchen doorway. Although apparently deaf to everything else in the world, he always somehow magically managed to appear downstairs within minutes of their mother arriving home, especially when she had been shopping. 'Oh, good!' he said, making for the carrier bags. 'Did you get Twiglets?'

'And what have you been doing, I wonder? Watering the television? Weeding the roof? Oiling the guinea pigs? Taking the piano for a gentle stroll down to the shops?'

Mr Sharp turned towards the children, cunningly hiding a Jumbo-size bag of Twiglets. 'Has your mother gone quite mad?' he asked.

'I think she must have done,' said Dan. 'Mum, why were you calling that man Mr Potward? You remember who Mr Potward is, and he's *gone*. Gone forever.'

'That was *young* Mr Potward,' said his mother.

'Young?'

'The son of old Mr and Mrs Potward. Haven't you seen him before? They all came to visit one Christmas and we went over and had a glass of sherry with them. Weren't you there?' The children shook their heads. It sounded like the kind of social situation they would have taken extreme measures to avoid. 'And that was his wife with him just now – and the Potwards' daughter, and her husband.'

'You mean – they hadn't come to see if they wanted to buy the house and move in to it?'

'Of course not! They were just sorting out which bits

of furniture they wanted to keep so they can get on and sell the rest. Now. What's all this they were telling me about your father holding naked rock concerts in Potters Field?'

'So it was all a total waste of time,' said Lizzie, later. 'All that effort for nothing.'

'No it wasn't!' said Max. 'It was brilliant!'

A thought had been going round and round in Dan's mind ever since the conversation he'd overheard between his mother and Young Mr Potward. It was the kind of thought he knew he ought really to keep to himself. Any sensible person would. It was bound to lead to trouble. But it was such an interesting thought that he simply couldn't help himself.

'His name was Potward too!' said Dan.

'Yes, we *know* that, Dan,' Lizzie said with great patience. 'Mum told us. We were *there*.'

'But don't you see?'

'See what?'

'That spell you pretended to do. It spelled out the letters of POTWARD. You did it on the old Potwards, but it happened to him as well!'

Max got it before Lizzie did.

'He broke his ankle!' he said, gazing at Lizzie in awe and wonder. 'On the very same day. He said so. The magic magicked everybody called Potward! Lizzie is a really and truly proper witch!'

4

Fish

Lizzie bought a thick lined notebook with a black cover and a silver pen of the kind intended for use on black surfaces. On the cover she wrote, in spiky witchy italic script:

The Book of Spells
by
Lizzie Sharp

She decorated the rest of the cover with stars, pentagrams and mystical magic symbols of her own invention. It looked absolutely stunning.

Now for the spells! She opened up the book, took an extra-thin black felt tip, and wrote:

Accident (Non-Fatal) – Potward
Ingredients
1 Tomato (chopped)
1 Orange (chopped)
1 Apple (firmly chopped)
1 Pint Water
Dusting of Pepper
1 Teaspoon Rabbit Droppings (approx)
Pour water into cauldron and add chopped things. Boil and stir. Collect rabbit droppings in enchanted binding cloth and stir in until disintegrated. Season with

pepper. Pour potion into vial and sprinkle to the North, South, East and West, completing a Circle of Doom. Results guaranteed within 24 hours.

Underneath she added: Tested May 23rd (she remembered this because it was the day after her birthday) and two red ticks, one for each Potward whose person had been fractured by the power of the magic.

This was all very satisfactory, but after three or four days of admiring it, it began to occur to Lizzie that she didn't have anything to put on page two. It was hard to plan a career as a good witch when you only knew one spell, and the only thing that spell seemed to do was to break people's bones.

Perhaps, she thought, there was actually only one spell in the entire universe, and she knew it already. The only reason she'd thought of it in the first place was because her mind had been going: 'Spell! Think of a Potward spell!' and some other part of her mind had immediately obliged – by spelling 'Potward'. Maybe this was all you needed to know to cast a spell on somebody – but the actual effects of the spell depended on the intentions of the witch. That would be *real* magic. Maybe, if she'd done the exact same spell, but wished the Potwards nothing but happiness and good fortune, they'd still be there at The Briars, bounding with good health and cackling over their winning Rollover Lottery ticket.

She needed to experiment, but it was very difficult to think of a suitable person to experiment on. What was needed was this: a person on whom she could cast – or try to cast – a Good Spell, without having to worry if the whole thing went wrong and they ended up in hospital with a shattered collarbone or a few snapped ribs.

Maybe Dan would think of somebody. Lizzie had been sitting for ages and ages gazing at her spell book without getting anywhere, and she was starting to get restless. She went out to the landing, banged on the door of Dan's bedroom (where he was bound to be busy working on something), swung the door open and went in.

'NOOOO!' shouted Dan in horror. He had almost finished a perfect model Spitfire he'd been working on for the past three months, and there was glue and paint and water out ready to use, and a three-quarters finished 3-D jigsaw of the Eiffel Tower on a table just inside the door, and here was Lizzie tumbling in like a whirlwind with arms and legs all over the place. 'No, no, no! Out! Go! Out of here! Don't touch anything, go away, go anywhere! Out! *Mind that table!*'

'But I wanted to talk to you,' said Lizzie, somewhat deflated. She liked to make dramatic entrances, and had expected to be greeted like a celebrity, not like a road accident.

'I'll come downstairs,' said Dan, hastily putting the lids back on everything spillable and shooing Lizzie out of the room.

Down in the kitchen Max was sitting by the window, with Snowball, the most affectionate of the cats, curled up beside him purring in her sleep. Max was playing I Spy with Leela and Hercules Dumpling and watching for people. A couple of weeks had passed since the open-air party for the horrible grown-ups who had all turned out to be Potwards. Nobody else had come to look at The Briars that the Sharp children knew of, but of course they were out at school most of the day. Despite all Lizzie's plans for a surveillance rota, it was now only Max and the Dumplings who did any serious watching. Max could only half remember the reason why they were supposed to be watching in the first place, but he knew for sure that he didn't want to miss out on another opportunity to dance in the garden with a lampshade on his head.

Lizzie and Dan arrived and fetched themselves a Fanta each.

'I have a slight problem,' said Lizzie. 'I have made great progress in my studies of magic . . . '

'Oooh!' said Max.

'There's no such thing as magic!' said Dan, who had soon begun to regret his rash remarks. The *really* worrying thing was that now about a quarter of him actually believed that some kind of Potward magic had happened. But he would never, never, ever admit this, especially to Lizzie, who was showing signs of getting out of control. 'There *is* such a thing as coincidence,' he said firmly. 'Mrs Potward was due to fall over absolutely any day. The Young Mr Potward with the crutches was much too old to be doing his own exterior paintwork and so he fell off the ladder. None of it was anything to do with you. It was all coincidence.'

Lizzie gave him a black look. How magic did she have to get, before even her own blood relatives had faith in her?

'What's coincidence?' asked Max.

Dan tried to think. 'It's – it's like when you pick six numbers on the lottery and they're the right six numbers. It's just coincidence when that happens.' He could tell, even as he said it, that this was an extremely poor example of coincidence.

'Oooh!' said Max. So far it sounded to him as if coincidence and magic were very similar and extremely powerful.

'No,' said Dan. 'It's not really like that. It's like – it's like if you dreamed there would be a terrible thunderstorm that blew the roof off the house, and the very next day there just happened to be one. *That* would be a coincidence.'

'Oooh!' said Max, entranced, and now totally convinced that coincidence was a very special kind of magic which gave people the ability to see into the future.

'I give up,' said Dan. 'I can't explain it.'

'As I was saying!' said Lizzie. 'I have made *very great progress* in my studies. I have reached a point where I have a brand new spell to try.'

'Can I be your assistant?' asked Max, scrambling down from the window seat and leaving the Dumplings to finish off the game by themselves.

'Possibly,' said Lizzie. 'But what I really need is a victim.'

'Victim?'

'I mean – a subject. You see, this new spell is a *good* spell, but it hasn't been widely tested yet and I can't be

34

entirely sure that there won't be side-effects. So I need to try it out on someone who doesn't matter.'

'Oh dear!' said Dan. 'I see the problem. You've crippled the entire Potward family already. You've *run out* of Potwards.'

'Nathan Dursley!' said Max.

'Nathan Dursley?'

'He's in my class at school,' said Max. Nathan Dursley was absolutely the worst thing in Max's life. He was only four months older than Max but he was six miles taller. He had red hair and a face like a heavyweight boxer and he never let Max play in the football game during break or the lunch hour. He nicked Max's drink and crisps any time he felt like it and he called Max 'bogslime', and sometimes even 'gobslime' which sounded much the same but was somehow worse. He had never actually hit Max, but it felt very much as if it were only a matter of time until he did, and once he'd done it the first time he would probably do it every single day for the rest of Max's life. Max found it very difficult to explain this properly to his family.

'I know Nathan Dursley,' said Dan. 'Little kid. His brother's in my year. Ben Dursley.'

Max knew all about that. Nathan Dursley had told him several times about his big brother, who was always somehow lurking just around the corner waiting to kick Max's head in.

'And his other brother's in Year Six,' continued Dan. 'Jacob Dursley.'

'And his sister was in my class at junior school, but

after junior school she went to Tollington Hall so I don't know her any more,' said Lizzie. 'Rachel Dursley.'

Max looked from Dan to Lizzie and back again in deepening misery as Nathan Dursley's big brothers and sisters multiplied into an army.

'I still see Rachel Dursley,' said their mother, coming in from the garden with some freshly-cut parsley. 'She comes into the shop from time to time.' Mrs Sharp was the manager of a chemist's shop in Stonebridge, the nearest town.

'Really?' Lizzie's attention was caught by this. 'What does she buy?'

'That's none of your business!' said her mother.

'I know what she buys,' said Dan. 'Lipstick and eye make-up and glittery nail polish and daft things to go in her hair. Stuff to take nail polish and eye make-up off again. Maybe a sugar-free drink so she doesn't get *fat*.'

'I'm impressed,' said his mother.

'I didn't know you knew Rachel Dursley!' said Lizzie.

'I don't,' said Dan. 'Never even heard of her till just now. She's a *girl*. She's *thirteen*. What else would she buy?'

Lizzie threw a damp tea towel at him.

'No violence, now,' said their mother vaguely, before disappearing back out into the garden.

'*Nathan* Dursley,' said Max, firmly.

'Who?' said Lizzie, who was easily distracted.

'Nathan *Dursley*. You wanted someone to practise a spell on. Well, do it on him. He's not nice.'

Lizzie looked doubtful. 'I don't think I can use a little boy of seven for experiments.'

'Children's bones heal far more quickly,' said Dan, helpfully.

'Oh, please, go on, Lizzie. Turn him into a toad!' What was the use of having a sister for a witch if she wasn't going to do stuff like that? Max felt the pricklings of tears and rubbed his eyes very firmly to make them go away.

'Maybe one day,' said Lizzie, kindly. Poor little Max – he looked so disappointed. 'When I'm more completely expert. I'm really only an apprentice now, you know, and it's very dangerous to go round turning people into toads if you aren't quite sure what you're doing.'

'Really?'

'Just the tiniest mistake in the ingredients and instead of turning them into a toad they turn into a road!'

'Ohhhh!'

'And that could be terribly inconvenient if you were indoors at the time. Just imagine the traffic driving both ways through your classroom on top of Nathan Dursley.'

'That sounds all right.'

'Not if you'd got run over it wouldn't be.'

'This is the most ridiculous conversation I ever heard in my entire life,' said Dan. 'Even if all of the rest of it made sense, how in the world is Lizzie going to cast a spell on a little kid she doesn't even know at a school she doesn't even go to? She'd probably pick the wrong one. She'd probably end up turning some perfectly innocent little kid into a dual carriageway.'

'Well, you think of something, then!' said Lizzie.

'I don't go to the same school as you either,' said Dan. 'I don't know the same people you know. There must be somebody at your school you really hate. Who's your worst teacher?'

Lizzie's eyes slowly lit up as an idea took shape. 'Yes! Of course! Why in the world didn't I think of that? Fish!'

'Fish?'

'Fish!' Lizzie punched the air in jubilation. 'This will be just the best thing ever. I'll cast a spell on Fish!'

Lizzie was in Year Eight at Cross Keys School, and she would have been almost completely happy there if not for Fish. Fish was the most unpleasant teacher Lizzie had ever known and she taught her very worst subject (Physics).

Her name had actually, really and truly been Miss Fish until, in the middle of Year Seven, she married somebody with a very ordinary surname. For a while Lizzie's class, 8J, still referred to her as Fish; then one day somebody called her 'The Artist Formerly Known as Fish', and one of the boys changed it to 'The Fartist Formerly Known as Fish', which caused all the rest of the boys to fall off their chairs laughing. This led to a series of increasingly revolting and unrepeatable nicknames, all beginning with F. Even the very primmest of the girls, those girls who on other occasions would recoil and shudder in distaste at the coarseness of the boys, raised no objection. But Lizzie still thought that the original unadorned name, Fish, so cold, dead, scaly and lifeless, suited her the best.

Fish's seating plan was the cruellest ever devised. All her classes were forced to sit in alphabetical order, with boys and girls alternating. Every boy had nothing but girls for neighbours and every girl had boys. Nobody had anybody to talk to and everyone hated every minute of it, which was how Fish liked things to be. And whenever you had to work in pairs (which happened a lot, in Physics) all the pairs went boy/girl, boy/girl, boy/girl. It was torture.

Fish wore thick black-rimmed glasses and she had a hard white shiny face with the waxen pallor of a china doll, and when she got really really angry – which was seriously scary – two little red spots burned, one in either cheek. Because she was so cold and harsh the entire time, you didn't really get any warning when she went berserk and lost it altogether. Once she had screamed so loudly and for so long at Tom Butler, one of the bolder boys, that he'd broken down and cried. Scary. He'd only been doing the ordinary sort of mucking around, and Fish just suddenly went mental. There was no kind of a bad thing you could do to Fish by magic which she wouldn't richly deserve.

Lizzie explained all of this to her brothers while preparing the cauldron and assembling the ingredients.

Max had been trying very hard to work out what the ingredients would be. FISH. There were lots of things which might be the 'S'. but the other letters were far from easy, especially the 'I'. There seemed to be almost nothing that began with 'I', except for ice cream, and Max thought that probably counted as two words, like the rabbit droppings.

Lizzie, however, set about mixing her potion without seeming troubled by this. In went a large amount of Ribena, an equal quantity of lemonade and a generous slurp of tomato ketchup. She then selected a withered-looking apple and orange – just exactly like the last time! – chopped them up and tossed them in to boil.

'That isn't going to spell "Fish",' said Max. Dan was writing notes.

'It isn't supposed to,' said Lizzie.

'I know why,' said Dan, scribbling some letters, looking at them and crossing them out again. 'It's because she isn't called Fish now. She got married and she's called something else.'

'Well done, that boy,' sang Lizzie, prancing over to examine the spice rack. 'Go to the top of the class. Do not pass GO. Do not collect two hundred pounds.' She took out a jar marked 'Nutmeg', and sprinkled some of the contents into the potion, which was bubbling away furiously, a violent and lurid shade of red. 'And we know the new name is the right one to use, because it worked just fine on Mrs Potward.'

'This teacher formerly known as Fish. She's called Mrs Ratklon,' said Dan.

'She's called *what*?'

'Ribena,' said Dan. 'Apple, tomato ketchup, lemonade . . . or maybe Mrs Lankrot.'

'That is not correct,' said Lizzie, 'and anyway I haven't finished yet.' She picked up the salt cellar.

'Can I do a secret ingredient, please?' asked Max, who was feeling distinctly left out. Lizzie looked at him.

'I did last time, and it worked out all right. Please?'

'All right,' said Lizzie. Max's face lit up like a sunbeam. She thought for a few moments, before bending down to whisper in his ear.

Max nodded, and scampered out of the room. Thump, thump, thump, went his feet up the stairs.

'You'd better not take too long, or Mum'll be back,' said Dan.

Lizzie glanced at the kitchen clock. 'I've got at least half an hour.' On Tuesdays Mrs Sharp finished work at half past five, and it took her at least fifteen minutes to drive home.

'It'll take half an hour to clean that pot!' said Dan, leaning over to look inside the cauldron. The contents simmered nastily.

Thump, thump, thump, came Max back down the stairs with their mother's bottle of Rosemary and Juniper Frequent Wash Shampoo (for fine flyaway hair).

'Shampoo?' said Dan. He went back to the table, picked up the pencil and wrote down 's' by the other letters.

'Sorcerer's Frothing Crystals,' said Lizzie, swirling three generous squeezefuls into the potion and stirring vigorously. A pinky-orange foam began to appear around the sides. It looked absolutely wonderful.

'OK,' said Dan. 'The teacher. She's called Mrs Snotlark.' This reduced Max to helpless giggles.

'I wish!' said Lizzie. 'And now – the final ingredient!' She opened the fridge door and began to rummage in its nether regions. 'Ah – here we are. Just the thing! Poisoned Fungus!'

41

Dan and Max could smell the Poisoned Fungus even before they saw it. It was a very old lump of that nasty blue cheese which only grown-ups eat, which looks as if it's mouldy even when it's brand new and which stinks of rot and decay. This particular piece had been lying around for some considerable time, and the cellophane wrapping was furred over with dense patches of blue mould.

'In it goes!' said Lizzie cheerfully, and, holding it by the wrapping, she tipped it right into the middle of the potion. The Poisoned Fungus seemed straightaway to combine with the Sorcerer's Frothing Crystals in a very lively chemical reaction; huge gaseous bubbles began to appear, and the pinky-orange lather rose a further inch. Occasionally a bubble burst with a gentle *glup* noise, giving off the most appalling stench.

'Cheese,' said Dan, and wrote down a 'C'. 'Her name is Mrs Crankslot.'

'Nope,' said Lizzie.

'Mrs Slantrock. Mrs Rantlsock. Mrs Snortlack?'

'You've got the letters wrong,' said Lizzie, looking over his shoulder. 'Where did you get the T from?'

'Tomato ketchup. That was the T and the K.'

'That was just K for ketchup. And most of those names you've written down wouldn't work anyway. The T and the K would have to be together. Like the RD in Potward. That's how it works.' Lizzie tipped the potion through a funnel into the empty lemonade bottle. It didn't all fit. There was almost enough left for another bottleful.

Dan crossed out the T and began again.

'Her name is Mrs Snackrol.'

'Mrs *Snack* roll?' Max had only just recovered from Mrs Snotlark.

Lizzie was distracted by the remainder of the potion. 'What am I going to do with the rest of this?'

'Throw it away, for heaven's sake,' said Dan. 'And then start washing up. Quickly.'

'I can't *throw it away*!' said Lizzie, horrified. A whole vial of potion, mixed to perfection? She might need it again someday. She might need it again next week. She opened the fridge, found a nearly empty bottle of Coke, poured the Coke down the sink and filled the bottle with potion.

'Mum'll find it,' said Dan. This was almost certainly true. Their mother always found everything. 'And she'll find that shampoo of hers the instant she gets in.'

Lizzie sent Max off to return the shampoo (thump, thump, thump), thought for a minute, and then opened the drawer where her mother kept Post-it Notes. These notes were bright yellow with a sticky band across the top, and her mother left them everywhere, with messages on, telling people what to do. She had once bought a pad of pink Post-it Notes for their father to use for the same purpose, but he just somehow couldn't seem to get into the swing of it.

Lizzie wrote on the top Post-it Note, in thick black felt tip: 'Lizzie's Biology Homework. DO NOT DISTURB!!!'. She stuck the note to the bottle, screwed the top tight shut and put it back in the fridge.

'There!' she said. 'It's an experiment in fermentation.'

Dan was reluctantly impressed. Lizzie never stopped to think things through properly before charging headlong into one of her crazy ideas, but she was tremendously good at improvising when the inevitable problems arose. Not only had she successfully disguised the potion, she would no doubt get all sorts of undeserved credit for doing her homework as soon as she got home and labelling it so carefully.

'Anyway,' he said. 'What's her name? Mrs Locsnark? I give up.'

'She's called Mrs Clarkson,' said Lizzie. 'And when this spell gets to work on her, she's going to be in *hospital*!'

'Hang on one second,' said Dan.

'Yes?'

'I thought you said this was going to be a *good* spell. And that the only reason you were trying it on this Fish Clarkson woman is because you were worried about the side-effects. I mean – not that it will do anything to her at all, because all of this is nonsense. But that's what you *said*.'

It was true. *Damn*. Lizzie had been having so much fun that she'd completely forgotten why she started this spell in the first place. It was supposed to bring good fortune to the subject. *Damn*.

She twisted the cap tight shut on the potion. She couldn't cast the spell until school tomorrow anyway. She was an extremely powerful (apprentice) witch, and by that time she would have thought of the perfect plan. Maybe she could have it both ways. That was the *ultimate* in power.

5

Parrot Sticks

Max was not happy with his life. Lizzie had gone off to school with a vial of magic potion in her bag, and Max was going to miss the whole thing. He wouldn't be there for the casting of the spell (and he knew how! He'd done the first one with her!) and he wouldn't be there to see the results. And meanwhile Nathan Dursley continued to rampage unscathed; that very day he nicked Max's drink and three-quarters of a packet of Starbursts at breaktime. Max began to wonder if he knew enough to cast a spell on Nathan all by himself. Maybe anybody could do it. Or maybe it ran in families, like red hair.

These were such interesting thoughts that Max found it hard to concentrate on what Miss Parrish was saying in the classroom. His eyes wandered around the room and his mind tried to invent spells. 'Dursley' was too hard; he just couldn't do the 'U' at all, but he could think of spells for Robert Crane, and for Jamie Bolton, and... 'Max! Pay attention! What *is* the matter with you today?' Max snapped out of the dream, but a few minutes later he was thinking of a spell for Miss Parrish (pizza, apricots, Rolos, reindeer)... 'Max! Are you listening? Max!'

After school you had to wait in your classroom until you were collected. Max usually stayed right at the back of the room until whoever was coming for him that day arrived. Nathan Dursley and his friends hung around by the door, in order to escape as soon as possible. They thumped each other a lot, and if they got the chance they thumped anyone else who got within thumping range. Fortunately for Max, he was nearly always collected after Nathan Dursley had gone, or else he would have probably been thumped every day as a matter of routine.

'Behave yourself!' Miss Parrish shouted in vain. 'Nathan! Robert! Alex Matthews! Is that your bag? Whose is it then? *Whose*? Well, give it to Natalie, then! Nathan and Robert, stop fighting! Robert, you need to wipe your nose. *Not on that!* Natalie, there's no need to cry, look, here's your mummy. Hello Mrs Francis, yes she's fine, nothing to worry about, just a bit over-tired I think. Peter, leave Robert alone! Stop that. I said stop that! *Nathan Dursley!*'

This happened every single day, accompanied by choruses of 'Sorry, Miss', 'I wasn't doing anything, Miss', and 'It was him, Miss!'

Max watched from a safe distance, hoping as usual that whoever was picking him up wouldn't be early.

'Nathan, here's your mother,' said Miss Parrish with obvious relief. Max peeked over towards the door to try and catch a glimpse of Nathan's mother (obviously he wouldn't have a *mummy*) but all he saw was a colourfully sleeved arm which reached in, grabbed Nathan Dursley by the back of his collar and removed him from the classroom.

Max tiptoed over to the classroom window and

looked out. He could now see the whole of the person with the colourful sleeve – a large, formidable-looking woman with a mass of dark red hair. This must be Mrs Dursley. She was surrounded by a group of children, all of whom seemed to be battling for her attention. There was Nathan; right behind him was a bigger boy with the same red hair, which runs in families (possibly like magic), and who must be Jacob Dursley from Year Six. In that case the slightly smaller darker-haired boy was Ben Dursley from Year Five. Mrs Dursley still had hold of Nathan by the collar, and with her other hand she held firmly on to a sturdy-looking little girl who was unmistakably a Dursley. She must be too young to have started school yet, or Max would have seen her around the place, but she looked to be already as big as Max, and no doubt she'd be starting in September, which was hardly any time away. Max could imagine it now: 'My sister's going to beat you up at break!' Nathan would say, and this girl from the Reception class would stomp over wearing a great big heavy pair of boots and kick him to pieces, with the whole school standing round laughing. Things didn't get much worse than that.

'Earth to Planet Max,' said a voice in his ear. Max jumped in shock. 'Anyone at home? Any signs of intelligent life?'

It was Dan. 'You shouldn't sneak up on people,' said Max reproachfully.

'Sneak? We've come to collect you. We've been here ages. Don't you know what day it is?'

Max often didn't know what day it was, but his dad

was here, across the other side of the classroom, talking to Miss Parrish (which was a very bad sign), and all in all he thought it was probably Wednesday. On Wednesdays Lizzie went to drama club after school and Mum picked her up when she finished work.

'Everything OK, Max Pax Sugar Smacks?' his father asked as they headed out through the playground to the car. 'Miss Parrish seemed to think you weren't exactly on top form today.'

'Oh,' said Max.

'Is anything the matter? Is anyone bothering you at all?'

'I'm fine,' said Max.

'What about that whatsisname Dursley?' asked Dan. 'The little one. Didn't you say he'd been giving you problems?'

'Nathan Dursley,' said Max, who wasn't at all sure that this was any of Dan's business. But it was too late.

'What's this boy been doing, Max?' asked his father.

'Nothing much,' said Max.

'Has he hurt you at all?' They had reached the car, but his father just stopped walking and carried on the conversation right there on the pavement.

'No,' said Max. Apart from the pushing and shoving at the end of school (which happened to everybody, and didn't count), the only injuries Max had ever suffered at the hands of the Dursleys were in his own imagination. But his dad was still standing there, waiting, and clearly expected to be told something. 'He took my drink at break,' said Max. 'And my sweets.'

'He took them? What do you mean, he took them?'

'He just took them!'

'He took them while you weren't looking?'

'No,' said Max, miserably. Nathan had in fact simply removed the drink from his hand and the Starbursts from the pocket of his shorts.

'But didn't you say, sorry, those are mine?'

'No,' said Max. What would the point have been? Nathan would simply have taken them anyway. At least this way Max retained some sort of dignity. From a distance it might almost look as if they were friends and sharing a drink, and that Max was looking after Nathan's Starbursts for him because Nathan had a hole in his pocket.

'But Max, look, this is no good at all. You have to stand up for yourself!'

'I can't fight Nathan Dursley,' said Max. 'He's bigger than me.'

'You don't have to fight him! Just say, very firmly, "I'm sorry, you can't have those, they're mine." And turn and walk away. That's all you have to do.'

Turn and walk away! Max tried to imagine doing this – walking away, unable to see what was happening behind him, unable to defend himself against the inevitable attack. Unable to tell whether he was going to be pushed over, smacked round the back of the head, or sent tripping headlong by a sudden sharp foot snaking round his ankles. He knew he wasn't brave enough. He knew that brave was generally considered to be a very good thing to be, but he just wasn't made that way. He was *nice*. He wouldn't have minded *sharing* his Starbursts, with Nathan and with everyone. He just didn't want to have to fight for them.

His father gave him a long, concerned sort of look. 'Do you want me to have a word with Miss Parrish?'

'No!' said Max, desperately. 'Everything's fine, Dad, really it is. I can manage. Let's go home.'

Dan, who had said nothing more, gave Max a sympathetic look as they clicked their seat belts shut. For a moment Max wondered if Dan ever had problems like his. Probably not – Dan wasn't *small* like Max. Dan had always been the proper sort of size for his age. But somehow, even as he thought this, Max knew that getting picked on wasn't anything to do with how big you were. It was about how big you felt inside.

When they got home their father made them carrot sticks and cheese slices so they wouldn't starve to death before tea time. Dan, who was a very organised sort of person, took his with him and sat down to get his homework done straightaway.

Max was too young to have homework. He took his plate outside and sat in the sun on the front garden wall, followed by Bonnie, sniffing hopefully for scraps. The only food Bonnie had ever been known to refuse was cucumber. Spat-out cucumber was a very unpleasant thing to clear up. Max fed her a piece of cheese, which disappeared in a single gulp.

Opposite, The Briars stood closed and empty, the For Sale sign looking more and more forlorn, weeds pushing up through the long grass in the untended garden. How in the world was Max to discover the secrets of magic? He knew Lizzie had a Book of Spells, because he'd seen the cover, all decorated with mysterious silvery witchy signs. But he had no idea what was inside, as Lizzie had shooed him out of her room before he could take a peep.

Lizzie had, however, dropped some hints as to the way things worked. The casting of spells seemed to be closely connected to the spellings of the names of things, which made sense. And if it was true that a very small mistake could change a toad into a road, then it seemed that things with very similar names were connected to each other. This also made sense. Their ingredients would be almost the same. Maybe it only took a very small amount of magic to turn something into something else, if the two things only had one letter different in their names. Maybe it was a spell which could be cast even by someone with such limited skills as Max, provided that magic ran in his blood. He took a bite of a carrot stick, and thought deeply.

Carrot, he thought.

And then a magnificently brilliant thought came into his head. Parrot!

It was almost exactly the same word! Maybe – just maybe – he could turn a carrot into a parrot!

Now there would be a truly amazing thing. He gazed at the remaining half a carrot stick, and tried to think logically. The thing that would make a carrot into a parrot was the letter P. All he had to do was add an ingredient beginning with P! He had one whole carrot stick left, but it didn't seem right to cast the spell on a carrot stick. You might end up with a parrot stick, which would not be nice.

Max went indoors and took a look in the vegetable rack. There was a perfect carrot there – a big, chunky carrot with a healthy green topping which you could just imagine being magically transformed into the colourful feathers on the head of a magnificent green parrot!

It was at this point that Max started to wish for an assistant. It would be so much more fun to do with two of you, and the moment the parrot appeared would be so vastly more amazing with someone else there to share it and admire Max's powers and remember it ever afterwards. Bonnie had followed him back into the kitchen, and was gazing up at him with that loving, longing expression she always adopted in the presence of food. But he didn't think Bonnie was at all a suitable assistant for an enterprise such as this. Supposing – just supposing – it worked, and all of a sudden, the carrot he held in his hand turned – *kazamm! kazoo*! – into a squawking, and no doubt very shocked, little parrot. It seemed all too likely that Bonnie would dive in and snap it up with a single CRUNCH. The picture of Bonnie spitting out the few pathetic feathers that were all that survived of the parrot was so tragic that Max felt close to tears at the thought of it. And it would be all his fault!

There was absolutely no point in asking Dan. When Lizzie did magic, Dan would come and watch and stand on the side and make sarcastic comments and shake his head, but Max just knew he wouldn't do that for him. He would say there was no such thing as magic, and not to be so ridiculous.

What was needed here was somebody who believed in Max, and who would agree with everything he said, and would be dumbstruck with admiration.

It was time to summon Roger Dumpling.

Roger was the most normal of those Dumplings currently existing. Hercules Dumpling had an impressive number of super-powers, but they were not the kind of powers that would be helpful on this occasion. They were excellent powers for fighting aliens, climbing up the sides of buildings, and diverting lethal asteroids on a collision course with planet Earth. They were ideal for situations when you wanted a lot of sparks and fireballs and things going ZAP! and POW! in brightly flashing colours. But this wasn't anything like that.

Leela Dumpling was if anything even less suitable. She was a great sport and always very interesting company, but you couldn't avoid the fact that she was an extra-terrestrial who had been switched at birth with the Dumplings' real baby (who was called Lola, and who was currently lost in outer space being raised by extra-terrestrials). Leela was very unpredictable and had an unfortunate tendency towards bossiness. There was absolutely no telling what she would do in the presence of terrestrial magic, but Max felt almost certain that whatever it was, he would lose control of the situation.

Which left Roger.

Roger Dumpling was an ordinary cheerful little boy with tousled brown curls, mischievous blue eyes and a dash of freckles. He enjoyed doing all the same things as Max did, and he agreed with pretty much everything Max said. He was the ideal companion.

'We need something beginning with P,' said Max to Roger. They discussed this for a while. There were plenty of things beginning with P, but they weren't things you could easily add to a carrot. There were potatoes, peas, peanuts and parsley, pineapple, pears, popcorn and pasta (several kinds). None of these seemed quite right.

'We could try pepper,' said Max. Roger didn't seem wildly enthusiastic about the idea of pepper, but he agreed to give it a go. After all, it had worked perfectly in the Potward spell, which was more than you could say for any of those other things.

Max reached for the pepper mill. He had never actually used it before, and it wasn't at all obvious how it worked. There was a knobbly bit on top which he pressed and tried to pull and turn, but it didn't seem to do anything. He shook it as hard as he could, but nothing happened. Then he remembered – Lizzie had just gone *twist twist* over the cauldron and a huge black cloud of pepper had flown out. He twisted the top and pepper fell out of the bottom in a dusty sprinkling on the floor. Roger did not look impressed. Bonnie sniffed the pepper, yelped in disgust and left the room.

Max put the carrot on the table and covered it in pepper. The pepper smelled horrible, and nothing happened to the carrot.

'This isn't right,' said Max. Roger agreed. You

couldn't really mix something solid with a carrot. Maybe a liquid would work better; the carrot might soak it up. Max opened the fridge, and there, right before his very eyes, was a Coke bottle with a yellow Post-it Note stuck to it. 'Lizzie's Biology Homework. DO NOT DISTURB!!!'.

Max and Roger looked at each other, and: 'Potion!' they both said together. It was perfect. It was already magicked by Lizzie, and it began with P! They would just borrow the tiniest bit. Just a few drops. In fact – and now Max's confidence was growing by the moment – just a few drops sprinkled to the North, the South, the East and the West, completing a Circle of Doom!

Max took the vial of potion in one hand and the carrot in the other, and raced outside, Roger trotting obediently behind. They went up the path at the side of the house and stopped halfway along. Max gave the vial a good shake and unscrewed the cap. The potion frothed up and whooshed out of the bottle, splashing the carrot (and Max's shoes) with a fizzing pinky foam. This was excellent. 'Abracadabra!' said Max. They repeated the process at the back of the house and at the other side. Whoosh! Fizz! Abracadabra! This was real magic!

And finally, back again at the front of the house, Max paused for a second. This was it. In five seconds he would have his very own parrot. He would call the parrot Polly, and she would live with him for the rest of his life. She would sit on his shoulder and whisper in his ear. Whoosh! Fizz! He shut his eyes, and hoped and wished with all his heart.

Abracadabra!

Nothing happened.

At least, nothing happened to the carrot.

But behind him, something began to happen in Cleve Road.

6

Torture Time

Max had been concentrating so hard on his parrot spell that he totally failed to notice the car which had been approaching down Cleve Road. The idea of the parrot rapidly flew out of his mind, to be replaced by less pleasant but much more urgent matters. If that was Mum and Lizzie back already, he was in *deep* trouble. But it wasn't their car; it was a white one, unknown to Max. This did not necessarily mean that he wasn't in deep trouble anyway.

The car pulled up and four people got out. There were two women; the one in glasses was admittedly rather sour looking, but the other one, who was blonde and snappily dressed in a blue suit, seemed OK so far as Max could tell. There was one man (ordinary). The fourth person was a girl of about Dan's age, who had long frizzy honey-coloured hair loosely held back in a ponytail, carried a school bag and wore a school uniform dress and blazer which Max didn't recognise. The girl gazed over at him with interest.

'Hello!' said the blonde woman, waving at Max. Max waved back, puzzled – did this woman know him? He didn't recognise her. He didn't recognise any of these people. He didn't always remember grown-ups but he was pretty sure he would have remembered the girl. But then the blonde woman crossed over the road to The

Briars, went up the front path and unlocked the door, and all four of them disappeared inside the house, the girl sneaking one last look over her shoulder at Max, his carrot and his potion.

Suddenly the whole situation became clear. These weren't people he knew at all. The blonde woman was just one of those chirpy friendly people who said 'Hello' to children even if they were total strangers. These people had come to look at the Potwards' house to see if they wanted to live there. This time they were the real thing! Max wasn't quite sure how a family with two women of about the same age fitted together, but at least they were a family and they were looking at the house. And Lizzie wasn't here to supervise. Max decided to go and fetch Dan, straightaway.

Dan had finished his homework and loaded up his favourite game, *Metropolis*, on his PC, which was his dad's old PC and which Dan had inherited (Lizzie had been offered it first, but she had opted for some complicated deal whereby she got a new tape deck and CD player and the computer passed down to Dan). *Metropolis* was one of those games where you designed and ran your own city, and it was wickedly addictive. Dan's city, which was called Triangula, had a population of 3,427 and had won the award for Most Orderly City two years running. He was currently trying to deal with a very nasty outbreak of fires in the built-up area in the south-west. The fires were his own fault – he'd been trying to save money on the firefighters' salary and they'd all gone on strike. It was a highly tense situation, demanding his entire concentration, and it was unbearably frustrating, at that very moment, to hear his brother repeatedly calling his name from downstairs.

He had promised to keep an eye on Max, so he was even less pleased to find him standing in the hall clutching Lizzie's vial of potion, now half-empty (how was he going to explain *this*?) and with quite a considerable amount of the missing potion staining his trainers bright pink (how was he going to explain *that*?). He wasn't even going to think about the carrot.

'Max, what have you done? Lizzie's going to be absolutely furious!' He hustled Max into the kitchen. Max was babbling something about parrots and people and pepper and potions and Potwards, and making it sound as if it were all Roger Dumpling's fault (that old trick!).

There was pepper spilled all over the kitchen floor. Dan sighed. OK. One thing at a time. First things first. 'Be *quiet*,' he told Max. Max closed his mouth in mid-squeak. Dan got out the dustpan and brush, swept up the pepper and tipped it into the bin. He squirted the room with pine-scented spray to hide the peppery smell. He had a close look at the carrot and then threw that in the bin as well. He could see just by looking that there was nothing he could do about the trainers.

'Now. What on earth were you doing with this? And don't try to tell me it was Roger Dumpling. Those Dumplings are nothing but trouble.' He took the potion from Max. Max had only intended to use the tiniest amount, but the level in the bottle had actually fallen by a good five inches.

'I was trying to do a spell,' said Max miserably.

'A Clarkson spell? This is a Clarkson potion.' There was no point trying to explain to Max that it was just a mixture of random ingredients. He simply wouldn't have taken any notice. Better to use arguments that made sense within the rules which Max believed.

'Just a spell.' Max hadn't really thought about the details, but he could see now that Dan was right. He hung his head dejectedly. He was lousy at magic, he'd wasted Lizzie's potion, he'd ruined his trainers and he was going to be in trouble with *everybody*. It was rapidly turning into the worst day of his life.

Dan looked at the potion bottle for a few moments. Then he got out the Ribena, and, very very carefully, tipped Ribena into the potion bottle until the level was the same as before. It took up most of the Ribena that was left, but when it was done you could hardly tell the difference.

'Will the potion still be a Clarkson potion? Will it still work?'

'It will work exactly as well as it did before,' said Dan, stowing the bottle back in its old place in the fridge (miraculously, Max had managed not to stain the label). 'It's just got a bit more "R" in it.' Something moving outside the kitchen window caught his eye. 'Who are those people out there? What's that car?'

'I was trying to tell you, but you wouldn't listen,' said Max. 'They're people come to look at the Potward house. I didn't know what to do. Should I take my clothes off and wear a lampshade?' Max didn't much like the idea of doing this with a young girl present; particularly one with such an inclination to stare.

'*No!*' said Dan, in tones of faint desperation. It seemed that as fast as Dan sorted out one crisis, Max was intent on creating a new one. It was all Lizzie's fault, for filling his head with this magic nonsense. He had never been any trouble before. You could leave him unsupervised for hours and he'd just invent some sort of game with those wretched Dumplings. And now look!

Outside, some sort of problem seemed to be developing. Dan could see a man walking slowly down the path of The Briars with his arm around a woman in a white blouse, guiding her along in that clucking concerned manner that people use when someone is ill. The woman's face was almost as white as her blouse. Possible medical emergency! Dan had always had a deep-seated yearning to dial 999, and here was just the faintest ghost of a chance of doing so – in a situation which did not involve any damage either to members of his family or his own home. This woman was able to walk, which was disappointing, but really she didn't look at all well and you never knew your luck.

'We'd better go and see what's happening,' he said. Max followed him outside, and Bonnie followed Max. (Roger Dumpling had slipped silently away at the sight of his old enemy, Dan.) Lucy, the most inquisitive of the cats, was already seated on the garden wall washing her left front paw and observing events.

The woman who was ill had now been put into the car. It was not possible to see if her condition was deteriorating. On the path stood a woman in a blue suit, fumbling in her handbag. And in front of the car, swinging a bag, was a girl, whose eyes met Dan's in a bold gaze of curiosity.

'Erm,' said Dan, to the girl. 'Is there anything wrong with your mother? Can we help at all? Our phone is just inside in the hall.'

The girl dragged her bag over to their front gate. 'That's not my mother. That's Elaine. She's not well *again*. It's the heat. It's always making her not well. She *swoons*. And in the mornings she's *sick*.' The girl wrinkled her nose. 'Ooh, is that your dog? Hello! Oooh, you're gorgeous!' Bonnie wagged her tail with enthusiasm. 'Can I stroke her?'

Dan opened the gate and the whole conversation moved out onto the grass verge outside. Bonnie set about licking the girl's hands as if she had never loved anybody so much in her life.

'Right,' said Dan. 'So – *that's* your mother?' He nodded towards the woman in blue, who had by now produced a mobile phone from her bag and was engaged in conversation. The last, fragile hope that he might get the chance to call an ambulance faded and died.

'No, that's Louise. She's an estate agent. She's calling the office. My mother lives in Whitfield with Roy who's my stepfather. Elaine's my stepmother and she lives with my dad in Stonebridge. She's expecting twins in November. And so the house isn't going to be big enough any more and we have to find a new one.'

Dan was somewhat taken aback by this onslaught of information. He knew this type of girl; there were several of them in his class at school. They had lots of hair and plump cheeks and they were called Olivia or Rebecca or Imogen or Emily, and all they did from the moment they got up till the moment they went to bed was talk, talk, talk, in a whirling cascade of perpetual babbling excitement and thrill. Words formed in their mouths with every breath that their lungs took, and there was almost no way known to mankind of stopping them. Usually this posed no problem to Dan since they went around in twos and threes, talking at each other. Normal people could just ignore them altogether. He hadn't encountered one on her own before. He wasn't at all sure that they should be *allowed* out on their own.

Max however was always happy to talk to anybody. 'So are you going to come and live here? Have you got any brothers and sisters?'

'I've got one grown-up stepbrother, one little half-brother and now there's these twins coming,' said the girl. 'And no, we won't be living here. Elaine didn't like the house. She said the kitchen was hopeless, it needed ripping out and doing again from scratch and they can't afford it. Elaine wants a house that's old outside and all new inside. She said that house is like a museum inside. Did anybody live there before?'

'There was this really horrible old couple,' said Max. 'But my sister cast a spell on them and they went away.'

'*Did* she?' The girl seemed impressed. 'I wish she'd

63

cast a spell on Elaine and make her go away. Having her for a stepmother has completely ruined my life.'

'She might do,' said Max. 'I could ask her, if you like.'

Here we go again, thought Dan. 'No you can't,' he said firmly. 'She's booked up solid for the next six months.'

The man across the road had been conferring with the estate agent woman. Now apparently he was ready to move on. 'Rebecca!' he called. The girl pulled a face. Rebecca! thought Dan. Typical! 'Come along, now. Elaine's feeling a bit better and we've got three more houses to look at before dinner.'

'Torture time,' said the girl Rebecca, raising her eyes to heaven. 'Got to go.' She gave Bonnie a last hug and reached down for her bag – which, Dan noticed all of a sudden, had her name inked on it in felt pen.

'Oh – let me take that for you!' he said, and, seizing the bag, he walked Rebecca over to the car, apparently deep in conversation. Max stood and gaped.

'What was that all about?' he asked, when the car had driven off.

'About? All what?'

'Why did you go off talking to that girl? You don't *like* talking to girls.'

'Poor helpless woman needed her bag carrying for her,' said Dan.

This didn't seem very likely to Max. 'Lizzie will be really disappointed that she missed the people,' he said.

'I don't think we need to tell Lizzie about them,' said Dan, firmly.

'We don't? Why not?'

'They weren't important. They didn't like the house, did they? So they won't be coming back.'

'She'd want to know anyway.' Lizzie always wanted to know everything.

'What she doesn't know can't hurt her,' said Dan, darkly. 'Hey – tell you what. I'll play Chelsea v Man Utd with you till Mum and Lizzie get back.'

It was the best thing to happen to Max all day. Almost immediately he began to forget about the people. And, even better – the Chelsea defence (Dan) didn't really seem to have their mind fully on the game, and by the time their mother's car drew up outside, Man Utd were only losing 14–3 instead of the usual 25–0. Maybe things were looking up.

7

Sunburn

Lizzie's day had proved to be something of a letdown.

She'd bounded into school, a witch in full flow and bristling with the most terrible vengeance, potion secure and waiting to be deployed. However, when it came to the point of explaining all this to her friends, her courage for once failed her, especially as she was far from sure how the spell would turn out. She felt she would be running the risk of a certain amount of mockery and disbelief if she took anyone with her on the Circle of Doom. Best to do it by herself. There would be time enough to advertise her talents more widely when she had achieved a greater mastery of her art.

She had decided that the spell on Fish should be a Good Spell with Bad Side-Effects. This was possibly a rather complicated spell for such a new apprentice, but Lizzie had never lacked ambition. The whole situation positively hummed with fascinating possibilities.

Since this was a Good Spell, Lizzie decided to reverse the direction of the Circle of Doom by completing it in a clockwise manner. It would have been extremely difficult to complete the circle in either direction if she'd had to go round the whole school; there were bits of it round the side at the staff entrance where she wasn't allowed to be. Fortunately, though, the Science Block, which had only been built a few years earlier, was an entirely separate building, and it was within the depths of the Science Block that Fish lurked in her white lab coat, inflicting misery on all who went near. It was a fairly simple matter for Lizzie to slip away from her friends at break, saying she needed the loo, and to dodge out of the other door towards the Science Block, potion at the ready.

But Lizzie soon discovered – exactly as Max was to discover that very same day – that casting a spell is not very much fun when you're on your own. She felt slightly foolish, scuttling round the Science Block pouring potion to the North, the South, the East and the West. She found herself missing Max, who was just exactly the right person for this sort of thing. And without any grass to soak up the potion it splattered all over the place, leaving pools of pinky-red liquid like the scene of a massacre.

Still! The spell was cast. Now there was nothing to be done except to await the results.

The most immediate results were not promising.

They'd only been back home for five minutes when her mother noticed the vibrant new colouring scheme of her trainers.

'Lizzie! What have you done to your shoes? They're – pink! They're ruined!'

'Um,' said Lizzie.

'Well?'

'Been out in the sun,' said Lizzie. 'They've got sunburn.'

'Don't be ridiculous!'

'It happens!' said Lizzie. 'I saw it on TV. On *Watchdog*. Thousands of angry consumers have been ringing in to complain.'

Max and Dan were standing across the kitchen, looking sheepish. There was a distinctly strange atmosphere. Lizzie had the feeling that interesting things had been happening in her absence. Max gave a tiny gulp. Their mother whirled round to look at him.

'I don't believe it!' she shrieked. 'You as well!'

Max as well?

'Your trainers!'

Max's trainers?

'Sunburn,' whispered Max.

Max's trainers had turned the exact same deep pinky colour as Lizzie's own. Lizzie stepped forward in disbelief to examine them more closely. It was – almost – as if Max had been there with her when she cast the spell. She remembered wishing he had been there, just for a few moments. But wishing didn't make it happen. Unless – unless, she was by this time so mighty a witch that even wishing for somebody's presence summoned them invisibly to the spot. The image of a spectral Max magicked by Lizzie into the puddles of potion was suddenly very vivid indeed. Lizzie reeled at this new and unexpected demonstration of her power.

'Ribena,' said Dan.

'Ribena?' Their mother looked from Max to Dan to Lizzie, and back again.

'He spilt it,' said Dan. 'It was an accident. I cleaned it

68

up.' Dan *had* cleaned up after Max's spillages, so it was only the very tiniest of untruths, and it would probably save a lot of trouble. He had expected Lizzie to leap for the fridge to check her second bottle of potion when she saw Max's shoes. Well, not to leap this precise moment, because with Mum there it would rather give the game away. But Lizzie hadn't so much as glanced at the fridge. Nor was she glaring at Max, which he had also expected. She was just standing there looking starstruck. He couldn't work it out at all.

Mrs Sharp tutted in exasperation, opened the cupboard where the Ribena was kept and took out the bottle. There was hardly a drop left.

'That's very careless of you, Max,' she said. 'Do you know the price of shoes these days?'

Max didn't know the price of anything except Smarties, Crunchie bars and bubble gum.

At that moment their father appeared in the doorway, beaming.

'Wrote a whole chapter today!' he said. 'Just finished this very minute. It's going really well!' He looked around. 'Is something wrong?'

'Hmmmph,' said Mrs Sharp. 'Just look at these children's shoes!'

'Oh dear!' His face fell.

'You may well say oh dear!'

'What happened?'

'Max seems to have spilt Ribena everywhere. But Lizzie wasn't even here at the time! I can't make any sense of it, and I'm too tired to try.' She opened the drawer, took out her pad of yellow Post-it notes, wrote on the top one:

Remember to Buy:
Trainers (Max and Lizzie)
Ribena

...stuck it to the fridge door, and swept out of the room.

'Oh dear,' said their father again. Everyone looked glum. There would probably be dozens of yellow Post-it notes pasted around the place in the next few days. This was always a very bad thing.

'These were falling apart anyway,' said Lizzie, removing her trainers. 'Look!' A piece of rubber sole flopped loose.

'And mine were too small,' said Max.

'I tell you what,' said their father. 'Put both pairs in a plastic bag and dump them in the bin so your mother never has to see them again. It's best that she isn't reminded.' Max and Lizzie scrambled to obey. 'I'll pour her a glass of wine and take her out to sit in the garden for twenty minutes. She'll have forgiven you by tea time.'

After their father had left the room the three Sharp children stood for a few moments in silence, looking at each other. The atmosphere was heavy with secrets, brooding, mysteries and unspoken thoughts.

'So, Max,' said Lizzie eventually.

Max felt a distinct sense of approaching doom.

'I know you didn't really spill Ribena on your shoes.'

Max looked at her.

'Do you – actually – remember anything much about it? The moment your shoes got stained?'

Dan, standing outside Lizzie's range of vision, frowned at Max, shook his head and mouthed 'No'. He had no idea why Lizzie should think Max was suffering from amnesia, but it seemed like the kind of delusion that should be encouraged.

'No,' said Max obediently. He was beginning to feel that there were altogether too many things he wasn't supposed to be telling Lizzie, and which he was supposed to forget about. If he carried on talking to her he was almost bound to remember one of them by accident, and it would be out of his mouth before he'd remembered to forget it again.

'*Well*,' breathed Lizzie. 'That is just so amazing.' She sat down, as if too dazed to support her own weight. 'That is *spectacular*, Max.'

'What is?' Dan was, by this time, in possession of quite a lot of information that was not available to Lizzie, but he could make no sense whatsoever of her current behaviour.

'It was the Clarkson potion,' said Lizzie. 'That was what stained Max's trainers.'

Max and Dan knew this already.

'Even though we weren't in the same place,' said Lizzie. 'That's how powerful the magic was. That's how good I've got already.' Lizzie was starting to tingle with the excitement of it all. If she really, really could make things happen just by wishing them – the possibilities were just too enormous even to imagine.

'Did you do your Clarkson magic spell?' asked Max.

'Of course I did!'

'Oh, tell us about it! Did you do the Circle of Doom and everything?'

'Of course.' Lizzie described the casting of her spell around the Science Block.

'And what's happened to Mrs Fish?'

'Nothing's happened to her *yet*,' said Lizzie. 'I only did the spell today. Even the Potward spell didn't work until the day after. We've got double Physics first thing tomorrow, as it happens. We'll see how things are going then.' She felt quite perky at the thought, which was not at all her usual reaction to Double Physics First Thing on Thursdays.

'What's it going to do to her?'

'Absolutely anything I want!' said Lizzie, glowing with newly-found invincibility. 'It will be basically Good, but the side effects could be really very unpleasant indeed. I'll work out all the details this evening.' She was looking forward to this. She would write it all down in her spell book, on a nice clean new page, in the darkest, most menacing black ink.

'I know what that Clarkson spell does,' said Dan casually.

It was Dan's turn to be the subject of two very puzzled stares.

'What on earth do you mean?' asked Lizzie. 'How can you know? You don't even believe in magic.'

'Maybe you're such a dazzlingly good witch that you've started to convince me,' said Dan.

Lizzie thought he was being sarcastic as usual, but there was a slightly unfamiliar tone to his voice, and she couldn't be entirely sure.

'But even so,' she said, uncertainly. 'I'm the witch. I'm the one with powers. There's no way you can possibly know anything about that spell.'

'I think maybe I have powers too,' said Dan mysteriously.

'Magic does run in families!' said Max, brightening. It was true! Here was the proof! It was a bit disappointing that the magic should show itself first in Dan, especially when Max had wished and tried so hard for special powers himself. But then again – if Dan, who was surely the least magical person in the world by temperament, had inherited the gift, Max's own powers, when he grew into them, would surely be unstoppable.

'This is just plain nonsense,' said Lizzie. For a moment she sounded exactly like Dan.

'You're saying magic is nonsense?' asked Dan.

'No! But you aren't magic! Anyone can tell that!'

Dan smiled serenely.

'All right then! Go on – prove it! Tell me what the spell does!'

'I can't reveal that at this moment,' said Dan. 'The knowledge might corrupt the spell.' He was enjoying himself very much. Max was gazing at him with the same kind of open-mouthed wonder that he usually saved for Lizzie, and Lizzie wasn't liking any of this one bit.

'Write it down and hide it away in a secret place!' said Max.

'He won't dare,' said Lizzie, loftily. Of course he wouldn't dare.

'Write it down? That's a really good idea,' said Dan. 'Anybody got some paper and an envelope?' Lizzie's jaw dropped.

'I'll get some!' said Max. He raced up the stairs to his room and got his Simpsons Stationery set, which had been a Christmas present. Max never actually wrote letters, so there was plenty left.

'Excellent!' said Dan. He took one sheet of paper and one envelope (both bright yellow). 'Anyone got a pen?'

Lizzie opened her schoolbag wordlessly, unzipped her pencil case and passed a pen to Dan, who went over to the far side of the kitchen, turned his back on them and began busily writing. Lizzie watched in darkest suspicion.

'There!' With a final flourish, Dan put the pen down, folded the sheet of paper in half, placed it inside the envelope, licked the seal and pressed it closed. 'All done!' He came back and sat down at the table. 'Just one last thing,' he said, and carefully signed his name along the left side of the envelope flap, so that half of the writing fell on each side of the seal. 'Just in case anybody was thinking of opening it up, having a look and sealing it up again in an identical envelope. Or steaming it open. Or anything.' It would be impossible to tamper with the envelope without the seal and the signature being damaged. It would still be possible to open the envelope, read the contents and then transfer them to another yellow Simpsons envelope – but it

74

would then be necessary to forge Dan's signature along the seal of the new envelope. And Dan knew quite well that Lizzie couldn't forge his signature. She'd tried many times before.

Lizzie glowered. She had had every intention of sneaking a look inside the envelope at the very first opportunity.

'It's not fair,' she said. 'It stops anyone else from opening it, but *you* still could.'

'Why would I want to open it?' asked Dan.

'To cheat! To change what you put!'

'It's hardly the sort of thing I could cheat at, even if I wanted to,' said Dan. 'It's not as if I can go and look up the answer somewhere, is it? Still, if it makes you feel happier, *you* sign the envelope as well.'

Lizzie took the pen and wrote 'Elizabeth J. Sharp' in a very fancy script along the right side of the envelope flap.

'When do we open the envelope?' asked Max. He had been half hoping that they might suggest that he added his own signature, but he could see that there wasn't going to be enough room, especially with Max's handwriting being so big and so wobbly.

'As soon as the spell has taken effect, I should think,' said Dan.

'How will we know when that is?' asked Max.

'*Lizzie* will know,' said Dan. 'She is a witch, after all!'

8

Conspiracy

Lizzie got up the next morning feeling extremely put out. What was Dan playing at? There was absolutely no way in the world that he could know the result of the Fish Clarkson spell when Lizzie did not even, at this moment, know it herself. And then – there had been that strange atmosphere in the house when she had arrived home from school. She had tried questioning Max, who could usually be relied upon to spill any secrets that were lurking. But Max had refused to be drawn into conversation. Whenever she'd tried to pin him down, he'd mumbled, 'Dunno', or something equally vague, and slithered out of the room. Max was usually absolutely delighted when anybody wanted to talk to him, so this was in itself all extremely suspicious.

Nor did her powers of making wishes come true appear to be very effective. She tried a few things at random while she was getting her school clothes on. She wished for her duvet cover, which was currently an ancient pinky-orangey affair, to turn jet black with a scattering of mystical silver stars. She had in fact seen the exact duvet she wanted when they'd all been out shopping last weekend, and an unfortunate wrong turning in Westalls department store had taken them through the dreaded Bedlinens and Soft Furnishings. It was particularly unfortunate because it reminded their mother that she'd been thinking of getting new curtains for the front room, which caused a lengthy and tedious delay while she fingered fabrics. Lizzie tried to turn the situation to her advantage by dropping a lot of heavy hints about the star-spangled duvet – which was absolutely perfect for an apprentice witch in every way – but of course nobody took the slightest notice.

She stared down at the old duvet and wished and wished, but nothing happened. It might of course be that the magic was slow-working, and that when she got back in the afternoon the duvet would have darkened and the stars would be starting faintly to shimmer. What on earth would she tell her mother, if this happened? Lizzie thought furiously. She would say – she would say that her school was doing a Sponsored Duvet Swap for the Homeless. But somehow she doubted that it would come to that.

Setting her sights considerably lower, she wished for one of the cats to come into her bedroom before she finished dressing. This turned out to be more complicated than it.had at first seemed, because she had to leave the door open for them, which meant dressing in a very awkward corner between the door and the bed if she was to have any privacy. She rustled magazines and scratched the bedclothes and tried every way she knew to make interesting-sounding noises, but no cat appeared. She wished the wishes aloud and she wished them inside her head. Nothing. It was all very discouraging.

And at breakfast Dan was sitting there with the most

maddening *knowing* sort of expression. She could have strangled him.

'Double Physics first thing!' Dan said to Lizzie, smiling sweetly. Lizzie glowered.

'You don't do Physics, do you?' his father asked him.

'I meant, Double Physics first thing for *Lizzie*!'

'Recite my whole timetable, why don't you?' Lizzie snapped. 'Set it to music and go and dance to it in the garden, why don't you?'

'Are you still having trouble with Physics, Lizzie?' asked her father.

'I'm having trouble with Dan,' said Lizzie. Dan smiled a sweet soothing smile of pure innocence. It was enough to make you scream.

Due to Mrs Clarkson's sadistic seating system, Lizzie, who was the thirteenth girl in the class in alphabetical order, had to sit next to James Sadler, who was the thirteenth boy, in Physics lessons. This was obviously not ideal, but it could have been considerably worse. James Sadler was a little shrimpy boy who quite liked Physics. You only had to take one look at him to see that he was never going to give Lizzie any trouble. When they had to do experiments or practical work, which they always had to do in pairs, he did it more or less entirely by himself while Lizzie doodled and dawdled and daydreamed. She copied his answers in tests – being near the end of the alphabet, Lizzie and James Sadler sat in the furthest row but one from the front, which was very useful. Generally, she made the best of the situation.

Mrs Clarkson Fish was always there ready and

waiting in her white lab coat when Class 8J arrived first thing on Thursday mornings. She did not like a single second of Physics time to be wasted. It was only 9.15, but by the tense drawn look of impatience on her face you would think she had been standing there for hours, glancing at the clock, tapping her foot and devising ways to make 8J's life as unpleasant as possible. And woe betide anyone foolish enough to start putting their things away at the end of the lesson simply because the bell rang. 'THIS LESSON ENDS WHEN I SAY IT ENDS! DID I SAY THAT THE LESSON WAS OVER?' Then she'd keep on talking about Physics for another five minutes, making them all very late for their next lesson, so their next teacher would straightaway be angry with them as well, and that would somehow tip over into the *next* lesson in a sort of domino effect that often lasted the entire day.

This particular Thursday everything seemed much as usual, which was a disappointment. Whatever the effects of the spell, they clearly hadn't been powerful enough to prevent Fish from attending school; there she stood behind her table at the front, deathly white and grim-faced as ever. Nothing seemed to have happened to her at all; maybe the spell had gone wrong. Maybe reversing the direction of the Circle of Doom had not been a good idea. It could be – terrible, terrible thought – that instead of reversing the *effect*, it would reverse the *direction* of the spell, turning it back on the spellcaster. In which case Lizzie could expect to end the day in Accident and Emergency in a plaster cast.

Suddenly, the spell failing to work at all began to look like not such a bad option. In fact – and here would be another good thing – if the spell did nothing then this would prove Dan to be wrong. Whatever he had written down and sealed in that envelope, it had taken him much longer than anybody could take to write 'Nothing'. Although 'Nothing' was actually precisely what you would expect Dan, who didn't believe in magic, to have written. In fact, now she came to think about it, it was impossible to imagine him writing anything else. Maybe he had written 'Absolutely nothing whatsoever because there's no such thing as magic', in which case not only would Lizzie's potion have failed but Dan would be right. This outcome swivelled back to being a very bad option indeed.

Round and round went Lizzie's thoughts in this gloomy fashion. It was as if she had a Circle of Doom of her very own, operating in her brain.

'Today you're going to do an experiment on the topic of density,' Fish announced by way of greeting. She had a clipped, robotic sort of voice, with the very faintest traces of an accent Lizzie could not identify, and with no expression in it whatsoever, except of course when she went mental and started screaming. The accent got a great deal more pronounced when she screamed. 'Turn to page 54 in your books. Work in your usual pairs.'

Class 8J flipped their books open. The experiment required them to put blocks of wood and of wax into glass jars containing water, brine and methylated spirit, and to record the results. Life didn't get much more exciting than this, for sure, thought Lizzie, idly twirling a pencil while James Sadler got busy measuring and pouring fluids. And guess what they would prove? Light things float and heavy things sink. World-shattering stuff. And just in case anybody didn't get the point, you only had to read on a few paragraphs in the textbook and it told you what happened in the experiment anyway. Lizzie did not consider any of this to be a useful way for her to spend time. James Sadler put a block of wax in the water and it sank slowly, eventually settling itself about an inch from the bottom. He added a block of wood, which floated on top. Lizzie wrote this down, which took fully ninety seconds. She wondered vaguely what wax would do if you boiled it up in a potion; now *that* might be interesting.

Fish's usual pattern of behaviour during practical work was to glide wraithlike around the room, generally following a sort of zigzag pattern matching the alphabetical layout of Class 8J, but occasionally making a silent and lethal detour to a site of suspected misbehaviour. There was almost nothing in life scarier than the moment when you realised that Fish was behind you, looking over your shoulder at the note you were surreptitiously writing to a friend under cover of your Physics book. This had not happened to Lizzie personally, but it had happened to her friend Tara Bywater, who had been too ill to come to school for three consecutive Thursdays afterwards.

Lizzie peeked out through a mass of frizzy hair to check on the current location of Fish. Not that she

(Lizzie) was actually doing anything wrong at the moment; the point was that she wasn't doing anything at all, and Fish was easily sharp enough to notice this kind of thing. ('Have you lost the use of all your limbs again, Elizabeth?')

But – and here was a very strange thing – Fish was still up at the front of the room sitting behind her table. She had not moved at all. She was sitting still as stone, eyes cast downwards. Her pallor, always extreme, had an altogether different tinge – somehow greenish, with a faint moist sheen. She looked – and suddenly Lizzie's spirits bounded – she looked *ill*.

All of a sudden the day seemed transformed. Fish was ill. She was too ill to be wandering round checking on people. She wasn't even looking at them. All Lizzie's doubts disappeared in a second. She had done it! Results within twenty-four hours! Two out of two – two potions, two successes. In fact, if you counted both the injured Potwards she had scored three out of two, which was more than a hundred per cent! And things were about to get even better. Suddenly Fish rose unsteadily to her feet and lurched towards the door by the blackboard, which led to a back room. She was through the door and gone so quickly that half of Class 8J didn't even know anything had happened, until they heard, from the room beyond, the unmistakable repeated gag-and-spurt sound of someone being violently, horribly, copiously sick. For a few seconds after the sound had ended, 8J sat stock still in stunned silence. Then a flurry of nervous giggles broke out, followed by some ripples of cheering.

Lizzie sat back, flexed her fingers and glowed.

Fish did not reappear for the rest of the lesson. Someone they didn't know turned up after about ten minutes and told them that Mrs Clarkson wasn't feeling very well and they were all to get on with some work quietly. By this time the class had rearranged themselves into a more normal formation, and the boys were busy breaking up the wax blocks into pellets and firing them across the room.

Sounds of mopping came from the back room; clearly Fish hadn't made it to the sink in time. Class 8J were helpless with laughter. Fish's breakfast, spattered in puddles all over the floor! Pure magic! By the time the bell rang for the end of the lesson there was a real carnival atmosphere in swing.

The rest of the day dragged by for Lizzie like a slow torture. If only she had had the confidence to tell people about the spell! It was a bit late to start claiming credit now. Damn, damn, damn. She was bursting with pride and triumph, and there wasn't a single person she could tell about it until school ended and she got hold of her brothers.

But to her horror, her mother pulled up outside the school with Dan and Max in the back of the car, and announced that they were all going into Stonebridge to buy new trainers. It would obviously not be sensible to start boasting about poisoning the Physics teacher with their mother present, so Lizzie had to grit her teeth and say nothing while they trailed gloomily round every shoe shop in town. Mrs Sharp was a thorough and relentless shopper. Eventually, as always seemed to be the way, they ended up back at the very first shoe shop and bought the first trainers they'd seen. Usually this sort of outing would include a stop for ice creams or cakes, but Mrs Sharp was still far too displeased about the trainer-colouring incidents to allow treats today.

Lizzie tried her best to flash meaningful glances at Dan, but Dan, who didn't need new trainers, sat there in the shoe shops in a world of his own, jabbing away at his GameBoy and paying her no attention at all. She poked him with her elbow as they dragged along the streets from one shop to the next (Dan wasn't allowed to play with the GameBoy on the move, not after the famous incident when he was so busy fighting a fifth-level boss that he walked SPLAT into a tree). But Dan just flashed back that same serene, wise smile she'd had to endure at breakfast. It was enough to drive you crazy. Max, meanwhile, looked completely out of it.

And when they arrived home, her *father* trotted downstairs with exactly that same mysterious smile of secret knowledge.

'Afternoon, everybody!' he said, with what Lizzie could only describe as a sort of suppressed glee. 'Afternoon, Lizzie!'

'Why me in particular?' said Lizzie, suspiciously.

'Dear dear,' said her father, with a chuckle. 'Don't bite my head off. Got out of the wrong side of the bed today, did we?' He seemed to find this last thought especially funny.

Lizzie began to suspect a conspiracy.

'We're going out to feed the chickens,' she said firmly.

'What, all of you?'

'All of us!' Lizzie ushered her brothers out into the back garden.

'What's going on?' she hissed.

'Going on?' said Dan. 'Isn't it us that's supposed to be asking you that? All the time we were out shopping you were acting like you were bursting with something.'

'Well, I thought you just might be interested to know that my Clarkson Fish spell worked!'

'Well, I sort of knew that already,' said Dan airily.

'You what?'

'It worked? What happened to her?' asked Max, who had completely forgotten about Lizzie's spell until that moment. Another difficult day of avoiding Nathan Dursley had put it out of his mind altogether.

Lizzie and Dan were staring at each other, both with a 'go on, then' look on their faces. Neither seemed to be prepared to say it.

'Tell us, Lizzie, please,' said Max.

'Oh, after *you*,' said Lizzie to Dan.

'After *you*,' said Dan, politely.

'Don't be ridiculous!' said Lizzie. 'You don't even know what happened! You weren't there! If I go first you'll pretend you knew!'

'But I've written it down, haven't I?' said Dan patiently. 'I went first. I went *yesterday*.'

Lizzie had not expected this. She had expected a degree of confusion, leading to the reluctant opening of the yellow envelope, followed by her triumphant announcement about the glorious felling of Fish, and ending up with renewed respect and admiration all round for her unearthly talents. Possibly a mumbled apology, which she would of course accept with good grace. You couldn't really blame Dan for wanting to seem important. Of course he wanted to be magic too. You only had to look at him to know that he wasn't, but you couldn't blame him for wishing it.

But Dan was showing not the slightest sign of confusion, or indeed of impatience. He really didn't seem remotely curious to find out what her potion had done. It was – almost – as if he already knew.

'Dan's right, Lizzie,' said Max, seeing that this was going nowhere. 'It is you that ought to say.'

Lizzie gave Max a look that said 'Don't expect any favours from me for the next year and a half.'

'All *right*,' she said. 'Fish was ill! She was made ill by the spell right in front of my eyes in the middle of Physics! She went this revolting colour and her face was all slimy, and then she ran out of the room and she was sick absolutely everywhere all over the floor. It was revolting. You could smell it three rooms away. She was so ill she never came back. Probably she went to hospital. So, Daniel Joseph Sharp. Are you going to say that's coincidence as well? My second spell, and it worked within twenty-four hours just like the first one! So!'

'*Wow*!' breathed Max. Lizzie was the luckiest person in the entire universe. Not only could she do magic, but she'd actually managed to be there watching while one of her spells worked. Max would have given absolutely anything to see it for himself.

'So, Dan?'

'Pretty much what I thought would happen,' said Dan.

'What?'

'I said, pretty much what I thought would happen. Try and watch my lips when they move. I've said it twice now.'

He was bluffing. He had to be bluffing. Didn't he? Lizzie suddenly felt less certain. What was going on here? Could somebody in her class have a brother or sister in Dan's class, and they'd phoned him and told him? She was halfway through a mental check of known siblings before she realised how unlikely this was. Dan would have had to have phoned the person in his class last night and put them up to it, and the older brother or sister would have had to agree, and would have had to agree not to tell Lizzie, and someone in Dan's class would probably have needed a mobile phone, and – oh, it was just impossible! But anything else was *totally* impossible, so it had to be right.

Lizzie was a famously quick thinker, but even for her this was a tough one. Even *if* all that had happened, which would account for Dan knowing (if he *had* known, which could never be proved), he wouldn't have known last night. The yellow envelope. Could he have somehow switched the envelope? They had given it to Max to hide, Max being the uninvolved party. He'd tucked it away somewhere in his room. But. Lizzie was confident that she herself could find anything in Max's room in no more than five minutes. It would almost certainly be inside a book, and Max only had about thirty books. Dan could have found it that morning, nicked a spare yellow envelope and sheet of paper while he was there, taken them to school, re-written his prediction when the spy phoned through with the information, and forged her signature over the seal on the new envelope.

Ha! And one thing Lizzie knew for sure was that during the few minutes they'd been in the house, Dan had not been out of her sight. He would not have been able to replace the new envelope in the old hiding place. If she sent Max off to retrieve the envelope right this minute, Dan would be *finished*.

Unless – unless he'd been working in league with Max. And – come to think of it – Max had been behaving pretty weirdly for the last day or so. He was never any good at keeping secrets, especially not from Lizzie. Conspiracy! She would kill them both. They'd been really really clever, but she would kill them anyway.

So. Lizzie's brain rattled away furiously. What could have happened was that Dan had given the new envelope to Max in the car, on the way from their school to her school to pick her up. And Max would be under instructions to hide it back in his room at the first opportunity. And she had cunningly foiled this plan, by dragging them both straight out to the garden! Yes!

'All right,' she said at last. 'We'll all go up to Max's room right now this minute, and he can get the envelope out from its hiding place, and we'll open it and see what you wrote.' Got them! There was no possibility that either of them would be quick-fingered enough to switch envelopes under Lizzie's watchful eye.

'No,' said Dan. 'We can't do that.'

Ha! Now he was trying to wriggle out of it. 'Why not, Dan?' she asked sweetly. 'Do you need a little time to *prepare* things?'

'Oh, no, not at all,' said Dan. 'We can't open the envelope yet because the effects of the spell are not complete.'

'What?'

'Don't you remember? It was a *Good* spell. You said there might be bad side-effects, but basically it was Good.'

Lizzie kept forgetting this.

'The point is, it worked!' she said impatiently. The details did not, at this moment, seem terribly important.

'But you've only told us about the bad side-effects,' said Dan, reasonably. 'Whereas I wrote down all of it. The Good Thing *and* the side-effects. My incredible powers of magic, which are growing stronger by the minute, tell me that there is more to come.'

'You're not magic!' shouted Lizzie.

Dan smiled. Any minute she would be yelling at him that there was no such thing as magic, which would be really, really funny.

'Just wait and see,' he said.

Lizzie had had enough. 'Right,' she said. 'I know what's going on here. We'll just go and check on the envelope. Just to be quite sure that it's still there.'

She marched them into the house and up the stairs. But before they got as far as Max's room she saw something that stopped her frozen in her tracks.

The door to her own bedroom was still open, and Sapphire, the laziest of the cats, was curled up and snoozing on her bed, right bang slap in the middle of a jet black duvet covered with silver stars.

9

Fingerprints

Max was getting more and more confused. He was almost certain by now that Dan was playing some kind of trick, and he felt that if he could only remember all the things he was supposed not to tell Lizzie, he might be able to work it out. But however hard he thought, he just couldn't. Obviously he wasn't supposed to tell her about using her potion. That would have caused a terrible storm. But he couldn't see what that had to do with anything.

They had both been acting so very strangely in the garden. And then Lizzie had insisted that they get the yellow envelope out of its hiding place, even though they weren't ready to open it yet. Max felt a bit hurt. Did she not trust him to hide it away safely? Max was an expert hider. He had slipped it in between the pages of his Giant Picture Dictionary, where it would take years and years for anybody to find.

And then, on the landing on the way to his room, Lizzie had suddenly stopped still and stared into her room with an expression of total amazement, as if she'd seen a ghost or something. Max peeked round the door but all he could see was Lizzie's bedroom. Maybe part of being a witch was that creatures from another dimension became magically visible. Maybe she could now see the entire Dumpling family, in which case she might start to treat them with a little respect.

'Lizzie? What's the matter? Lizzie?'

Lizzie turned round slowly to face them but her eyes were focused somewhere off in outer space.

Max began to be worried. 'Lizzie?'

All of a sudden Lizzie snapped back to life. But it seemed that she snapped back into a completely different version of herself from the suspicious one they'd just been talking to in the garden. She had just the same starstruck expression as yesterday in the kitchen when she'd seen Max's trainers. She looked as if she'd just learned the biggest and most wonderful secret in the world.

'All right,' she said eventually, as if she had only just remembered why they were all there in the first place. 'Let's have a look at this envelope.' Her voice was different. It was almost as if she didn't think the envelope was important any more.

Max led the way into his bedroom, pulled the dictionary out of the bookshelf and showed them the yellow envelope.

'Happy now?' asked Dan.

Lizzie took the envelope and studied it, turning it this way and that.

'This does not appear to have been tampered with,' she said at last.

'Of course it hasn't,' said Max. 'We've been at school all day.'

'However!' continued Lizzie. 'Dan's behaviour has been extremely suspicious. If we don't open it right now, tougher security measures will be required. I think we should open it now. But that idea seems to make Dan nervous. Anyone would think he hadn't had an opportunity yet to do whatever he's planning to do.'

'How could I possibly do anything?' asked Dan, who seemed to be enjoying himself thoroughly. 'You've signed your name over the seal.'

'You could copy my signature,' said Lizzie. Everyone knew that Lizzie couldn't do Dan's signature, but it had never been tried the other way around. At least, not in public. Maybe he'd been practising in secret for years. That would be entirely typical.

'I know!' said Max. They looked at him. 'Fingerprints!'

'There's no point testing it for fingerprints, Max,' said Lizzie, for all the world as if this was something they did the whole time. 'We know Dan has handled the envelope. It wouldn't prove anything if his prints were on it.'

'You don't understand,' said Max. 'Put your fingerprint on the envelope. Even if Dan can copy your writing he can't copy your fingerprint. Nobody can. And Dan's got a fingerprint set he's had for ages and he's never even used it.' This was true. The fingerprint set had been a present the Christmas before last. It looked interesting, but never somehow quite interesting enough to open. Twice already their mother had tried to whisk it away to take to the charity shop.

'Excellent idea,' said Dan. Max beamed with pride.

'I know where it is,' he said. 'I'll go and get it.'

'No!' said Dan, horrified. 'Don't you dare go in my room.' He didn't like to think of the damage that might be inflicted on his Spitfire, which was only a couple of days away from being finished, if Max started rooting around in his things. '*I'*ll go and get it.'

Max looked hopefully up at Lizzie, It wasn't often he had a really good idea that nobody else had thought of first, and you'd think she might say, 'Well done', or *something*. But Lizzie was staring out of the window in a dream. It seemed as if she'd barely even noticed.

The fingerprint kit contained an inky pad, record cards for storing prints, some dusting powder and a magnifying glass. Dan was the sort of person who read the instructions right through before starting anything, and the first couple of record cards got ruined because he didn't immediately get the hang of taking a clean fingerprint without smudging. So it all took quite a long time. But in the end they managed to take a clear set of prints each, and Lizzie added her own prints to her signature on the envelope, which was now surely completely tamperproof. And then their father shouted to them to come down for tea, and there was a general rush to the bathroom to scrub all the ink from their fingers. Dan said Max could keep the fingerprint set if he liked, and Max hid the yellow envelope and the print records away inside the box of a Toy Story jigsaw (three pieces missing).

They had pizza for tea. Everybody liked pizza but serving it was always a major operation because they didn't all like the same things. Dan and his father weren't keen on peperoni, Lizzie claimed to be allergic to onions, and Max wouldn't touch tomato if it looked like a tomato (although he was passionately fond of tomato ketchup). Mrs Sharp was very partial to tuna but nobody else except Dan could even bear to eat a piece of pizza that tuna had once touched. This all meant that they had to cook three different pizzas every time, even allowing for mushrooms and olives to be exchanged at the table.

Max looked around. It seemed to him that his family were acting more and more strangely. Lizzie was on another planet. His father had a mischievous grin on his face, which Max had sort of noticed when they got home after shopping, but because the grin had seemed to be aimed at Lizzie he'd assumed it was yet another private joke he didn't understand. But now, his father was exchanging private grins with his *mother*, and they *both* kept sneaking expectant glances at Lizzie, as if they were waiting for her to say something. As for Dan, he'd been looking mysterious for a whole day now. There were quite definitely things going on all over the place, and Max didn't know *any* of them.

He didn't like it. Too much of people not behaving normally made him feel nervous. You had to keep a watch on things or else your whole life could go spinning out of control. He decided to have a go at Dan at the first opportunity. This turned out to be quite easy, because as soon as she'd finished her pizza Lizzie went up to her bedroom, announcing that she had to *think*. This caused a fresh outbreak of winking and chuckling between his parents.

Max cornered his brother in the living room.

'I need to talk to you, Dan.'

'Actually,' said Dan, 'I was thinking I probably needed to talk to you.'

This sounded unexpectedly promising. If Max could be part of just one plot, he was sure he wouldn't mind so much about the others.

'What's going on with Lizzie and the secret envelope and Mrs Fish being sick?' Dan looked at him. 'It is a trick you're playing on Lizzie, isn't it? You don't really know anything about magic?'

'It is a sort of a trick,' said Dan. 'Except not the way she thinks.'

'You're going to try and do something to that envelope, aren't you? You won't find it, you know. I've hidden it really well this time.'

'Not in a book, you mean? I expect it's in a jigsaw in that case.' Max's face fell. 'Anyway, it doesn't matter,' said Dan. 'I'm not planning to go near the envelope. It's just such brilliant fun watching Lizzie worrying about it.'

'It's more fun for you than it is for me,' said Max. 'Because you know what's going on.'

Dan admitted that this was probably true.

'You can't have really written down that Mrs Fish would be sick all over everywhere,' said Max. 'It's not possible. Did you?'

'I didn't use those exact words,' said Dan. 'But it says that more or less.'

This really couldn't be true. 'How can it say that? It didn't even happen till today.' Max felt that if he had to endure very much more of not knowing anything, he would probably explode.

'I can't tell you that right now. But look. I'll make you an absolute promise that after we open the envelope I'll tell you everything. As long as you promise you'll never, ever tell Lizzie.'

'But why can't you tell me now?'

'Because if I do you'll go around with it showing all over your face. You'll look as if you're bursting with a secret and you'll start to giggle any time anybody says anything about the envelope or about Clarkson Fish. And Lizzie will know. She always does. And she'll get you to tell. I'm sorry, Max, but it's true. It always happens. She only has to *threaten* you with the Tickling Torture and you'll tell her anything she wants to know.'

'But I want to know *now*,' said Max miserably. Even as he said it he could tell that it wasn't a very convincing argument. Then something better occurred to him. 'If you tell me afterwards then Lizzie will torture me afterwards just the same. You ought to tell me now so I've got time to practise not giggling. I could practise! I really can!'

Dan shook his head. 'If I tell you afterwards, it will seem natural for you to giggle. Anyone would giggle to think that I'd written down exactly what happened to Clarkson Fish and that Lizzie will never ever know how. It's the best trick in the entire history of the world.'

Max sighed. 'And you really will tell me?'

'I really will tell you. On one condition.'

'What's that?'

'You have to promise that when we open the envelope, if what it says inside reminds you of anything, you won't say. You have to say absolutely nothing at all.' This was in fact why Dan had also wanted to speak to Max. You could never be quite sure what Max noticed and remembered, and it was just possible that he might blurt something out and totally ruin the best moment of Dan's life so far.

'I'm not *stupid*,' said Max. 'I wouldn't have said anything.'

'It's not a question of stupid,' said Dan. This was probably a good time to chuck in a little flattery. 'In fact if I didn't think you were clever enough that you might suddenly start to work it all out on the spot, I wouldn't need to be worried, would I? But if you hadn't been warned you wouldn't *know* not to say anything.'

Max thought about this for a while. 'All right,' he said grudgingly. 'But you'll tell me straightaway afterwards? The very next minute?'

'As soon as Lizzie isn't there,' said Dan.

'Will it be tomorrow?'

'I don't know,' said Dan. 'I can't tell. Do you think I'm magic, or what?'

And with that Max had to be satisfied.

10

Name the Blob

Lizzie was lying stretched out on her magic duvet, writing furiously in her Book of Spells, the cover of which exactly matched the cover of the duvet. So much had happened in the last twenty-four hours!

She had started a new section to record Wishes. This was divided into two parts: Fulfilled Wishes (a hundred per cent success rate so far!) and Wishes Awaiting Fulfilment. This second list had already reached a second page; wishes had been tumbling into Lizzie's head faster than she could write them down. There were so many things she wanted! She already had a small television in her room but she could really do with a video as well, and a DVD player. She wasn't quite sure what this was, but she knew she wanted one. She wanted a Personal CD player (anti-shock, rechargeable) and several dozen new CDs. She wanted a mobile phone and an entire wardrobe of new clothes. She wanted tickets to see several bands live, a long weekend at Alton Towers and a fortnight in the Caribbean. She wanted to star in a film, probably with Leo DiCaprio (who would say she was the most talented actress he had ever worked with). She wanted her own bathroom (with jacuzzi), a pet snake and a Rolls-Royce with her own personal chauffeur. She wanted a swimming pool and she wanted to be on TV *absolutely all the time*.

Several practical difficulties were beginning to emerge. Lizzie was thirteen years old, with no income of her own and a mother who noticed everything. It would be hard to find explanations for the brand-new, top-of-the-range goods that kept mysteriously arriving – and those were just the *simple* wishes. She'd probably have to wait until she left home for the rest of them. It was too frustrating for words.

There had to be an answer. She would – now here was an idea – she would invent a very rich friend who had so much of everything that it was no trouble to her to lend lots of it to Lizzie. That would account for the smaller things. The friend would be called Tatiana Belinsky. Tatiana would never be able to come and visit Lizzie in person, because her family were so rich that they spent every weekend in Paris and the whole of the holidays on their ranch in California. And just in case anybody asked Lizzie's real friends about the elusive Tatiana, she would be a new girl in another year who Lizzie had met at drama class.

But Lizzie was quite sure she wouldn't be allowed to borrow things like videos and mobile phones, even if the unspeakably wealthy Tatiana had three of each. So where would they come from? From where could somebody of Lizzie's age possibly acquire such things?

She would win them all in competitions! Yes! Lizzie punched the air with glee. Not only was she a top-class witch, she was also quite clearly a genius. All she had to do was announce that her new hobby would be entering competitions. She would specify, each time she made a wish, that the desired item should arrive nicely packaged, and containing a letter from some magazine or TV show or radio station congratulating her on her win in their 'Name the Blob' competition or whatever. There were millions of these competitions and all of them were too easy for words. She might even actually enter some of them (and, naturally, wish that she would win). And everyone would just think she was the luckiest person in the world (which was of course true). Dan and Max would probably guess the truth but she would bribe them with lavish prizes.

All of this had rendered Tatiana Belinsky somewhat unnecessary, but she sounded so glamorous that Lizzie decided to keep her anyway.

Excellent! All sorted nicely. Lizzie now turned her attention to the Spells section, which was in need of updating.

Extreme Vomiting Potion – Clarkson

1 Orange (shrunken and mouldy)
1 Apple (withered)
Half Pint of Lemonade
1 Small Cup of Ribena
A Generous Portion of Ketchup
Sprinkling of Nutmeg
Sorcerer's Frothing Crystals (Three squeezings)
Poisoned Fungus
Boil liquids in cauldron. Add fruits and simmer until mushy. Stir in ketchup and nutmeg. Squeeze Frothing Crystals into mixture. When the foam has reached a height of two inches crumble in Poisoned Fungus and

leave to decay. Pour completed potion into vial and complete a Circle of Doom in a clockwise direction. Excellent results guaranteed within 24 hours.

She completed the spell notes with yesterday's date and a very large red tick.

It hadn't gone exactly as planned – but then, she had kept the plans deliberately on the vague side. It had turned out to be an entirely Bad spell. Maybe she could only do Bad spells. This would make a career as a Good witch rather difficult. But she could do Good wishes. They were positively her speciality. And maybe it was wisest to have a full range of products available. She would sell them on the Internet and become a millionaire.

She had completely forgotten Dan's prediction that the spell was not yet complete.

Max would have liked to carry on talking to Dan a while longer. It would be interesting to know if Dan had noticed all the same odd things as he had. But Dan had picked up the TV remote and switched on to a sci-fi serial on Sky, with the air of someone who does not wish to be disturbed.

Max didn't want to watch television. He wandered back into the kitchen, where his father was chucking pizza crusts into the bin and loading up the dishwasher.

'Hello there, Maxwell House,' said Mr Sharp. 'Looking for a job to do?' Max winced. 'Or just looking for company?'

'Just looking for company.' Max sat down on the window seat.

'It's a shame there aren't some young people living round here for you to play with,' said his father.

Max had been saying this all his life. 'I hoped someone with children was going to move into The Briars,' he said. 'We all did.'

'Early days,' said his father. 'These things take a long time. Even after you've found the house you want to move into, it probably takes another couple of months to get everything sorted.'

'But nobody's even started to move in yet. Have you seen anyone look at the house?'

'I haven't noticed anybody,' said his father. But then, he wouldn't.

'There were some people yesterday with a girl,' said Max. Was he supposed to be not telling anyone about that? He couldn't remember, and in any case it was too late now. 'But they didn't like the house. It was too big. The girl was too big as well.' Max knew that boys of his age were of no use whatsoever to ten-year-old girls.

'That's a shame. Maybe The Briars won't be easy to sell. It's a long way from anywhere else. Not everyone likes living out in the middle of nowhere.'

'So why do we have to live here?' asked Max.

'Price,' said his father. 'It's much much cheaper than living in the town. Out here we can afford a house this big. All three of you have your own bedroom. Huge bedrooms! If we didn't live here you'd have to share a room with Dan. Probably a room that was smaller than the one you've got all to yourself now. How would you like that?'

Max thought about it. It would in some ways be fun but probably in most ways not. Dan was so fussy about all his things, Max wouldn't be allowed to move for fear of damaging something. And he wouldn't be allowed to make a proper mess. And Dan went to bed an hour later than Max, and he'd wake him up. Actually, as often as not Dan spent that hour in his bedroom, which he wouldn't be able to do with Max there going to sleep. It wouldn't work at all well.

'Not very much,' he said. His father seemed to be in a conversational mood, so he took a deep breath and added: 'Dad, why were you and Mum giving Lizzie funny looks at teatime?'

'The strangest thing happened,' said his father. 'Would you like me to tell you about it?'

'*Yes!*' Max could hardly believe his luck. All of a sudden everybody was telling him things! He must remember to ask more questions in future. It obviously worked.

His father poured himself a mug of coffee and sat down at the kitchen table. 'I was going past Lizzie's bedroom this morning and for some reason the door was open, which is very unusual, don't you think?'

'Very unusual,' said Max. Lizzie's door had a big handmade sign on it saying 'Keep Out!' followed by details of the terrible fates that awaited anyone who disobeyed. Mrs Sharp took no notice of this whatsoever, but Max had been very careful since the time he barged in without thinking and caught Lizzie wiggling around in front of the mirror miming to some girl band song.

She had not liked this one bit, and his punishment had been memorably painful.

'And,' went on Mr Sharp, 'although I couldn't actually see Lizzie in there – I still don't know where she was hiding – I could *hear* her. She seemed to be calling one of the cats. And then, out of the blue, I heard her say how much she wished she had that black duvet cover with the stars on that she saw the other week in Stonebridge. Do you remember it?'

'No,' said Max.

'Well anyway, your mother and I had decided to buy it for her as a surprise present next time one of us was in town without her. She really does need a new one. So I thought to myself, I know what I'll do! I was meaning to pop into Stonebridge to buy a couple of books anyway, so I thought, while I'm there I'll buy the duvet cover, and I'll slip it on to her bed before you all get back, and I won't say a word! She'll be so amazed, I thought. It would be as if she made a wish and *alakazam*! it came true!'

Something began, very slowly, to go *click* inside Max's head.

'Don't you think that was a funny idea?'

Max nodded in silence.

'And the really strange thing is, she hasn't said a single word about it! Isn't that peculiar?'

Max gazed at him. 'Have you told anybody else?' He hardly dared ask.

'Well, I told your mother while you lot were all upstairs. We kept expecting Lizzie to say thank you.

Anyone would think she really believed it had appeared by magic!'

'Ohhhh,' said Max. All of a sudden he understood everything. Two different mysteries had been solved at once! And – here was the truly wonderful part – nobody else in the family had enough information to understand any of it themselves. It felt absolutely glorious.

'Dad.'

'Yes, Max?'

'Will you promise me something?'

'If I possibly can.' His father was looking amused.

'This is *serious*.'

'All right, all right. Tell me what it is that's so important.'

'Will you promise not to say anything about it to Dan and Lizzie? About buying the duvet? And ask Mum not to either?'

'Why ever not? Lizzie's bound to mention it sometime soon, you know.'

'I think she mightn't,' said Max. 'It's very complicated to explain.' He gave his father a beseeching look. 'Please? It's a kind of joke. I really can't explain it. Please?'

'All right, if it means so much to you.' His father smiled indulgently. 'You know I can't resist when you look at me like that with those huge brown eyes. But I want to hear this joke eventually! It sounds like a good one!'

Sometimes it was very useful to be only seven, and small for your age.

*

Dan was enjoying one of his favourite episodes of *Space Station Betelgeuse*. The Overlords had sent Bretzoid the Parthusian to investigate the site of the suspected wormhole in Sector 118. Unknown to them, Bretzoid had jumped ship on the party planet Hedonia, and was at this very moment dancing drunkenly in a 43-mile long conga line, while his spaceship hurtled on unmanned towards the wormhole. The Overlords were not going to like this at all.

The door opened and Max bounded in. 'I've got a secret! It's the funniest thing in the whole world!'

'Hush!' said Dan. 'I'm watching this. It's really good.'

Max looked at the television. 'You've seen this one before. It's *always* on.'

'That's why I know how good it is,' said Dan. 'Be quiet. It'll be finished in another ten minutes.'

Max began to do running headstands on the settee.

'Nooooo!' shouted Dan. Onscreen, the Overlords were about to arrive on Hedonia and extract a terrible vengeance from the unfortunate Bretzoid. 'Be quiet! Go away! Go away till this is finished.'

Max tipped himself over the back of the settee and slithered out of the room. Dan could hear him out in the hall, sitting pressed up against the door listening for the end titles of *Space Station Betelgeuse* to start playing. He hurled a cushion at the door. '*Go away*!' There was silence.

The programme finally ended, with some truly spectacular explosions. 'You can come in now,' yelled Dan. Max did a forward roly-poly into the room, sprang to his feet and perched dangerously on the arm of Dan's chair.

'I know a *secret*,' he said.

'Doesn't sound like it's going to stay a secret for long,' said Dan. 'Who in the world was silly enough to tell *you* a secret?'

'Dad told me. And it's a really really brilliant one.'

'So, are you going to tell me? Or did you just come in here to gloat?'

'What I thought was this,' said Max. 'I'll tell you this secret if you tell me the secret about Mrs Fish now instead of making me wait. That's *fair*. And if I giggle when Lizzie's around I'll be giggling about the other secret. And if she really does torture me I'll tell her the other one.'

'I can't believe you've heard another secret that would make you giggle at Lizzie.'

'I have! It's probably even better than yours!'

'You'd better tell me what it is, so that I can be sure.'

'I'm not going to tell you!' said Max. 'Did you think I was that stupid?'

Dan had rather hoped that he was that stupid. But there was no way he was going to agree to swap secrets when he didn't even know if the other secret – *if* it existed – was as good as his.

'Sorry,' he said. 'You'll just have to wait. It probably won't be long.'

As it happened, it only took one more day.

11

The TotalSortedZone

Next morning Lizzie was restored to her normal self, and in a great good humour.

'I've met this new girl called Tatiana Belinsky,' she said over breakfast.

Max spluttered into his Coco Pops. 'Tatiana Belinsky!' Nobody could really be called that. It was the funniest name he'd ever heard. 'Lizzie's got a friend called Tatiana Belinsky!'

'And I suppose Roger Dumpling is a *sensible* name,' said Dan.

'This is hardly the same thing,' Lizzie said rather sharply.

'It does sound rather exotic,' said her father. 'Is she Russian?'

'She's half Ukrainian and half Polish,' said Lizzie. 'And she's an only child and very very spoilt. She has every single CD in the world. She's going to lend me some. She might bring them to school today, she said.' Lizzie had made a lengthy and detailed wish before she came downstairs, sitting cross-legged on her magic duvet. She thought she had quite definitely felt the vibrations of the magic sparkling and crackling beneath her.

'That's nice,' said her father. Nobody seemed very interested in the untold wealth of Tatiana Belinsky.

Yet. The seeds had been planted.

In their mother's car on the way to school Lizzie asked to be dropped off at the newsagent on the corner of Taverton Road. She wanted to buy some magazines. Magazines were packed full of competitions and she needed to get a move on and plant that seed as well.

'But it's at least ten minutes' walk from there to your school!' said Mrs Sharp. 'You'll be late!'

'No I won't,' said Lizzie. '*You're* the one who's running late. You've still got to drop the boys and get to work. *I* am going to be early.'

'But!' said Mrs Sharp. Lizzie knew what she was thinking. Lizzie would never be seen again, and when the policemen arrived her mother would have to tell them that no, she hadn't dropped her daughter safely outside the school gates, she had dumped her in the street to fend for herself against abductors and aliens.

'Mum, I'm *thirteen*,' she said. 'You were going to school on the bus by yourself when you were eight. You're always telling us. When you were my age you had a husband and eight kids to support and you went down the coalmines every morning and you lived in a cardboard box in a hole in the road. We don't know how soft we have it, young people nowadays. Remember?'

'Well, just be careful,' said her mother, pulling up reluctantly beside the newsagent's. She peered worriedly down the road (checking for muggers and murderers) but in fact the only people to be seen were kids wearing the same uniform as Lizzie, straggling in twos and threes towards the school.

'I'll be fine,' said Lizzie, opening the door and darting out before her mother had time to think again. 'Byeeeee!' She zipped into the shop and perused the selection of magazines. They didn't like you to browse, but at this time of day there was a crowd of people from her school keeping the shop staff busy, buying chocolate and crisps to fend off pangs of hunger during the long dreary day ahead. Lizzie picked out five magazines: *Go Girl!*, *Supersonic Hits 2001*, *Wicked!*, *StreetLife* and *TotalSortedZone*. The cost of these knocked a bit of a dent in her ready cash, but money was very soon going to be the least of her problems.

She flicked through the magazines while she walked the rest of the way to school. Just as she thought – competitions everywhere. The prizes ranged from a signed Boyzone Frisbee (do me a favour!) up to a revolutionary 128-bit multiplayer P52 console (with five top games and a steering wheel!). This was going to be too easy for words. She would allow a week or so for the competition closing dates to expire, and another week's delivery time, and after that the goodies could start to arrive almost every day. Lizzie was entering the TotalSortedZone.

She'd dawdled so much that when she reached the school everyone had gone inside already. Oh dear. On Fridays they had Assembly for the whole school – it was the one day of the week when you couldn't slip in quietly without being noticed if you were late. Lizzie stuffed the magazines in the bottom of her bag – if people saw them they'd all start wanting to borrow them

111

to read, and she'd lose track of who had what straightaway, and probably never see them again. She pelted through the doors and swung into 8J's classroom just in the nick of time.

Lizzie's good spirits had evaporated by the end of school. She hardly said a word during the drive home. The minute they got in she raced up to her bedroom, but came back down a few minutes later with a very dissatisfied expression.

'Something wrong, Lizzie?' asked her father.

'Mmm-hmph,' said Lizzie. Her CDs, which she had taken such time and trouble to prepare the way for, had failed to arrive. She had expected that they would be sitting there smack in the middle of the duvet waiting for her, possibly with one of the cats purring contentedly alongside. And this was not the only blow that had been dealt to her magical powers today.

'I don't know,' said her father. 'You're up, down, all over the place!'

'I'm a teenager,' said Lizzie. 'I'm supposed to be moody. Remember?'

Her father heaved a dramatic sigh. 'How could I forget?' He had once worked out that there would be a period of six months when all three of his children would be teenagers at the same time. This was six years away in the future, but he had made his plans already. He had, he told them, taken out medical insurance to pay for the intensive psychiatric care he would certainly need if he was to survive. He had written the outline for a novel which, he said, would almost definitely require him to spend the whole six months doing vital plot research in Peru.

'Grrrmph,' said Lizzie, and Mr Sharp fled back upstairs to his computer.

'Any news of Mrs Fish?' Max asked.

Lizzie gave him a dark look. There was indeed news of Fish, and she wasn't at all sure that she liked it. She had spent much of the day trying to arrange the facts in a fashion that suited her, without great success.

'As it happens there is some news,' she said.

Dan raised an eyebrow.

'We had School Assembly today,' said Lizzie.

'I hope the news is going to get a bit more exciting than that,' said Dan.

Lizzie ignored him. 'And during Announcements, Mrs McManus said, "And now for some very happy news! Mrs Clarkson is leaving us at the end of this term!"'

'She didn't really say that,' said Max.

'Well, she almost did. The happy bit was supposed to be for her, not for us. She's leaving to have a baby!' Lizzie looked at them defiantly. She knew what they were going to say. They would say, 'Aha! So that's why she was sick yesterday. It wasn't anything to do with your spell. She was sick because she's having a baby and that sometimes makes people sick.' Lizzie had thought of all this and had done her best to prepare her tactics. 'So!' she said. 'In fact the spell worked perfectly! It turned out just exactly as I said for the victim. Good, with bad side effects. And all within forty-eight hours!' She knew even as she said it that it didn't really make sense. Fish must have been pregnant for months already. Although anyone must surely admit that the sickness and the announcement had happened remarkably quickly after the Sprinkling of the Potion.

'I'm impressed,' said Dan.

Lizzie looked at him with suspicion. 'You are?' This was not in the script.

'Clearly the spell worked just exactly as it should,' said Dan. 'The magic is very powerful. It's turned out just as I thought.'

'What?'

'Max.' Dan turned to his brother. 'It's time to open the sealed envelope.'

'Oh!' Max hadn't realised that this was going to happen. He raced upstairs and fetched the yellow envelope from the jigsaw box. The envelope looked incredibly battered and used, considering it had been brand new only two days ago. Nobody could doubt that it was the right envelope. There were Lizzie's and Dan's signatures along the sides of the flap; there were Lizzie's inky fingerprints.

Max had hoped to be allowed to open the envelope himself, but Dan tweaked it out of his hand immediately and waved it in the air with a dramatic flourish.

'And!' said Dan. 'The winner of the award for the Most Magic Person in the Universe is...!' He slit the envelope open with his finger. 'Dan Sharp! Yeah! I would like to thank all my friends and family and everyone who voted for me!'

'Give me that!' screamed Lizzie. She snatched the sheet of yellow paper, turned it right way up and read:

This potion makes you be very sick in the mornings and have baby twins. Recommended for women only.

Lizzie said nothing at all for a minute.

Max couldn't read the words. From where he was standing they were upside down. He moved round behind Lizzie. Now they were the right way up, but he couldn't read them anyway because they were in joined-up writing.

He couldn't bear it any longer. 'What does it say?'

Dan recited the words from memory.

'Oooh,' said Max. Dan shot him a very fierce glance, and Max remembered, just about in time, that he wasn't allowed to say anything.

'You cheated!' said Lizzie at last. Somehow, she had been tricked. The only other possibility was that Dan had inherited the same powers as she had. Which was out of the question. 'Anyway, you weren't even right. What's this about twins? Nobody said anything about twins.'

'It will be twins,' said Dan. 'It's a very ancient spell and it never fails to produce twins.'

'That's rubbish!' yelled Lizzie. 'You can't make babies by mixing potions! You know that!'

'Maybe you don't understand enough about magic yet,' said Dan. 'Just wait and see. It'll be twins. It's the Ribena that does it.'

'Oh!' Suddenly Lizzie turned to Max, who had managed not to say a single word, though he was thinking a great deal. 'You know!'

115

'I what?'

'You know what he did! I've had enough of this. I'm going to *make you tell*!' And without any more warning than that Lizzie grabbed him, kicked away his legs so that he collapsed on the floor, and began to tickle him very violently under his arms.

'No!' screamed Max. He buckled and fought and tried to kick out, but Lizzie had pinned his legs to the ground. 'Don't! No!' Max wailed, arms flailing, body arching, trying in vain to clamp his elbows to his sides.

'Tell me! Tell me and I'll stop!'

Max's face was turning bright red. 'I *don't know*!'

Lizzie carried on tickling. She pulled off his trainers and began to tickle the soles of his feet. 'Let me go!' screeched Max. 'I *don't know*!'

All of a sudden Lizzie loosened her grip and stood up. Max shrivelled into a shrunken ball like a deflated balloon.

'Don't think you've heard the last of this!' she said to Dan, and, tossing her head, she stormed out of the room.

Max lay whimpering on the floor for at least five minutes while he recovered. Even then he hardly dared move in case Lizzie was still standing there in deadly silence, waiting for him to expose some soft ticklish part of himself so that she could launch a fresh attack.

When at last he rolled over and looked around, he found himself entirely alone. This was really a bit much. You'd think Dan would have stayed around long enough to sympathise with him about being tortured when he was completely innocent, and to congratulate him for remembering to keep his mouth shut and for his extreme bravery.

He found Dan in his bedroom, applying paint with a ridiculously thin brush to the tail of the Spitfire. It seemed to Max that Dan had been working on this model for most of his life. It looked absolutely perfect.

Dan didn't look surprised to see Max. He heaved a resigned sort of sigh, wiped the paintbrush and put himself firmly between the Spitfire and Max.

'You might have stayed to see that I was all right,' said Max.

'I thought you were probably going to live,' said Dan, sounding if anything rather disappointed about this.

'Wasn't I brave? I didn't tell her anything!'

'You didn't *know* anything,' said Dan.

Max felt that this was hardly the point. Dan had played the trick and he had got away scot-free while Max had been tortured. He thought this deserved some recognition.

'So how did you do it?'

Dan sighed again. 'All right. I'll tell you. But you remember what you promised? You must never, ever tell Lizzie.'

'I know. I promise. Now *tell* me.'

'Okay. Do you remember a couple of days ago, those people came to look at The Briars? They had a girl with them who came over to talk to us, and there was a woman who wasn't feeling well.'

'Of course I remember.'

'And do you remember the girl talking about her stepmother, and how she was an absolute nightmare, and she was always being ill?'

Max's brow furrowed. It sounded familiar, but he hadn't been paying all that much attention at the time. His mind had still been occupied with the parrot spell he'd been trying to cast just before the people arrived.

'Do you remember why her stepmother was always being ill?'

Max couldn't.

'Rebecca said the heat made her faint and she was sick in the mornings. Because she was pregnant! She was going to have twins!'

'Twins!' Max paused to think. 'You mean Lizzie did the spell on her as well? But Lizzie wasn't even *there*. She was still at school.'

'You mean you still don't get it?'

Max thought some more. He thought and thought, and gradually it dawned on him what must actually have happened.

'Oh!'

'Isn't that amazing?'

It was more than amazing. 'But – that means I'm just as magic as Lizzie is!'

Dan stared at him in total perplexity. 'It means *what*?'

'It really must do. Because it was me who did the spell with the potion Lizzie left behind in the fridge. And then straightaway these people arrived in the car and the woman was ill and we found out why. And Lizzie took the rest of the same potion to school and cast the same spell on Mrs Fish. So you knew she would be having twins and be sick as well!'

'Noooooo!'

'What do you mean, Noooooo? You just said so!'

'I didn't say that at all! Max, you're talking total nonsense. It isn't a spell. There isn't any magic. The woman in the car *was Mrs Clarkson Fish*!'

Max was stunned into silence.

'*Now* do you understand?'

Max didn't understand. 'But it couldn't be,' he said. 'She's a teacher. She would have been at school, same as Lizzie.'

'Lizzie was at drama club,' said Dan. 'School had finished.'

'But you don't *know* Mrs Fish. You'd never even heard of her till Lizzie did the potion. How could you have known it was her?'

'Rebecca had her name written on her schoolbag,' said Dan. 'I only noticed it just at the last minute. I mean, why would I look at her *bag*? It said "Rebecca Clarkson" in big black letters. You could have seen for yourself if you'd looked. And I thought – hmm. Interesting. And so I picked up her bag for her and carried it over to the car.'

'I remember *that*,' said Max. 'I thought it was a bit strange.'

'And on the way I said, "That's funny, my sister's got a teacher called Mrs Clarkson, is it any relation to you?" And it just happened that it was her stepmother. She told me all about it. You have absolutely no idea how many words a girl like that can manage to say in one minute. I was exhausted just listening.'

Finally, Max understood. Just about.

'So you were never going to change the envelope at all?'

'Of course not. I *told* you that. It was right all the time.'

'But how could you have known that she would be sick during Lizzie's Physics lesson?'

'I didn't know. And I never actually said that she would be. But I did know Lizzie had double Physics first thing the next morning, and I knew Mrs Fish had started to be sick in the mornings. It was quite a good chance. It happened to work out perfectly. But everything I wrote down would have been true anyway.'

'But how can you possibly say the magic didn't work?'

'I don't believe this,' said Dan. 'I just explained the whole thing to you.'

'Just think about it.' Max felt a buzz of excitement building up inside him. 'I did the Clarkson spell, all by myself. With the Clarkson potion. I did the Circle of Doom and everything!' There was no need for Dan to know that parrots had been involved in any way. 'And the very next second there they were! A whole carful of Clarksons! Just like that!'

'Max, I've already told you that things like that are coincidence.'

As far as Max could recall, coincidence was Dan's word for anything that was even the slightest bit magical.

'You don't think it was weird?'

'Coincidences *are* weird. That's why they're coincidences. It's not really all that unlikely. They were looking for a bigger house. There's a big house for sale right opposite us. They probably came straight from picking the girl up from school.'

Max wasn't having this. 'It's just not true. Think about it. Two potions Lizzie's done and both times the same things happened. People with the name on the potion came here in a car and went inside The Briars. And the exact same people that she did the potions for, she got rid of forever. First the old Potwards and now Mrs Fish. How much coincidence is *that*?'

Put like that, it did all sound a bit much. Dan was starting not to like the way the conversation was going. Max was turning into a real arguer. It was time for a change of subject.

'Anyway,' he said. 'Now it's your turn.'

'My turn to what?'

'To tell your secret. That really good one Dad told you about Lizzie. You wanted to trade, remember?'

'I'm not telling you that,' said Max.

'What? But you have to. I told you mine.'

'But that wasn't what I promised,' said Max. 'I promised not to say anything when you opened the envelope and I promised never to tell Lizzie when you told me how you did it. That's *all* I promised. I didn't even know my secret then.'

Dan couldn't believe his ears. Usually you could do anything you liked with Max. He forgot things almost as soon as you said them and he chattered on like a drain.

And here he was remembering the most inconvenient things, and striking bargains, and sticking to his word, and not behaving like a baby at all. The atmosphere of secrets and magic – of secrets and *coincidence* – seemed to be changing him in the most unexpected ways.

'Fine!' Dan shrugged. 'Be like that. I'll ask Dad what the secret was.'

'He won't tell you! He promised.'

Dan knew this was true. He had tried asking already.

'You should have traded when I offered!' said Max, and with that he marched out of the room.

12

Another Dinner Ruined

Everything that was fun had finished and Max felt flat and dead as lead. The spells were over until Lizzie decided to do another one, and after the trick Dan had just pulled off, that might take *years*. He very much wished he could tell her the truth, but he had promised, and he couldn't break a promise. Maybe one day if Dan broke a promise to him, he would. Was that fair? He wasn't sure.

He had managed to find out every single secret, but he was starting to find that knowing secrets can get a bit lonely after the first thrill of discovery. Dan was in a bad mood with him and Lizzie was almost certain to be in a bad mood with everybody. And the house opposite stood there as dismally empty as ever.

'Dan's an incredibly crafty sort of person,' said Roger Dumpling, who was perched on the kitchen table, swinging his legs over the side. 'You're going to have to watch him really closely in future.'

'I know,' said Max. 'He works things out in his head and he doesn't say anything to anyone.'

'But he isn't magic at all,' said Roger Dumpling. 'Just tricky. That doesn't mean it doesn't run in the family, though. You are quite definitely starting to show signs of being magical. You cast a spell and bingo! it worked.'

'It was supposed to turn a carrot into a parrot,' said Max. 'But I see your point.'

'That wasn't really sensible,' said Roger Dumpling. 'Adding a P to a carrot wouldn't make it a parrot. You've still got a C left. It would make a Pcarrot. Or a Carprot. Neither of those is a proper thing so it couldn't be expected to work.'

'But it wasn't even the right spell. It was a *Clarkson* spell. I needed to make a mix of things that spelled Parrot. I bet that would have worked.' Max suddenly had a pleasing vision of a carful of parrots arriving to inspect The Briars.

'All on your own again, Maximilian the Ninth?' His father came into the kitchen, with a finished-work and ready-for-fun sort of air. 'Oh sorry, Roger, I didn't see you there.'

Max smiled. His father, who inhabited a world of imaginary characters himself, was the only member of his family who was properly aware of the Dumplings.

'I'd better get tea started,' said his father.

'What are we having?'

'Chicken and jacket potatoes.' Mr Sharp opened the fridge and delved into its depths, emerging with a family-size pack of chicken pieces.

'Can't we have chips?'

'When did you last have chips?'

'For lunch today at school,' Max said reluctantly. 'There's always chips on Fridays.' Max found school lunchtimes difficult, especially when there were chips. The chips disappeared very quickly and if you were at the back of the queue there wouldn't be any left. Max was not a good pusher or jostler and he was one of the smallest people in his year, so as often as not he missed out. This made him feel so miserable and helpless that he actually preferred days when there wasn't anything he specially liked.

'You'll turn into a chip one of these days,' his father said cheerfully. 'Now. Shall I do these on the barbecue?'

'No,' said Max, knowing quite well that nothing he said would make any difference. The whole point of the barbecue wasn't really about cooking food; it was that his father liked to play with it. Max much preferred his food cooked in the oven or on the grill. Barbecued food never tasted right or smelled right. 'They'll have black crispy burnt bits on.'

'Very nutritious,' said his father. 'Very good for the digestion.'

'And there's nobody here but us.' In Max's opinion barbecues were a party sort of thing. He could see that it was useful when there were lots of people visiting, to keep them in the garden where they couldn't cause too much trouble. 'And Dan is in a mood and Lizzie is in a mood. I wouldn't bother if I were you.'

'You're no fun at all,' said his father. 'A barbecue is just the thing to cheer people up. And it's a beautiful evening.' He wandered off outside to load the barbecue with charcoal, humming to himself.

'Another dinner ruined!' said Roger Dumpling, darkly.

'Jacket potatoes!' said Max, sadly. The potatoes would be charred black on the outside and shrivelled inside. Most of them would get thrown away. Perhaps he could use them for a potion of his own. Max knew that anything involving cauldrons and boiling was out of the question for him, but who was to say a *cold* potion wouldn't work? Perhaps he could mix up a parrot potion from scratch. The potatoes would do for the P, and every spell seemed to use an apple and an orange. He would need a lot of liquid to mash it all up and make it pourable, though, and after the incident with the trainers he couldn't possibly risk using Ribena. Still, it was an exciting idea. He would work on it.

There was a clattering on the stairs and Lizzie walked in, closely followed by her mother. Both had changed into T-shirts and jeans, and Mrs Sharp had a towel draped round her shoulders with which she was absently rubbing her hair dry.

Lizzie eyed Max as if he were a worm, and sat down at the other end of the table with a pile of magazines, some plain white postcards and a pen.

'I'm going to start entering competitions,' she announced. 'There are a gazillion competitions in all these magazines and I'm naturally lucky. I should do very well indeed.'

'I did read once that far fewer people enter competitions than anybody thinks,' said her mother. 'So your chances are actually quite good.'

'And they have them on TV too, all the time,' said Lizzie, encouraged. 'You phone in and give the answer and leave your name and number.'

'I know those,' said Max. 'It always says, please ask

the person who pays the bills before calling.'

'Quite right too,' said his mother. 'That person is me, and the answer is no. I expect it costs a fortune.'

'I should really have a mobile,' said Lizzie. 'Almost everybody I know has got one. Tatiana Belinsky's got two.' But her heart wasn't really in the argument; she would have a mobile of her own soon enough. Although the continued absence of the CDs she'd ordered was distinctly worrying.

Mrs Sharp made muttering noises about some people having more money than sense. 'Where's your father, Max, do you know?'

'Out lighting the barbecue,' said Max.

Lizzie groaned theatrically. 'I hate eating outside. There are always insects.' She began filling in a postcard for a competition called Name That Tune (three first prizes of 61-key Touch-Sensitive Electronic Yamasaki Keyboards with Synthesiser Function and Stereo Speaker!). The scene was all very *normal*, thought Max. Nobody mixing potions or muttering dark secrets or sealing mysterious envelopes. No Circles of Doom. You would never think that less than an hour earlier this room had been the site of a brutal and completely unjustified torture. Nobody was behaving like a stranger (although Roger Dumpling, who had no great reason to like Lizzie, thought it very suspicious that she had calmed down so quickly after the opening of the envelope, and that she was almost certainly up to something). But, just for the moment, you would almost think they were an ordinary family again.

This was not to last long.

Again there was the clattering of footsteps on the stairs – this time a more slow, measured tread. The footsteps came towards the kitchen and Dan stood framed in the doorway. In his hands he held, with great care and delicacy, a small model aeroplane. He had finally, after three months' hard work, finished his Spitfire. The last brushstroke of paint was dry. It was perfect.

Nobody looked; nobody realised. Mrs Sharp was whisking green things out of the fridge, ready to chop up into a salad. Lizzie was bent in concentration over the postcard she was writing, and Max was watching Lizzie.

Dan tiptoed slowly over to the kitchen table, nursing his precious creation. Never in his life had he spent so long working on one single thing. Never in his life had anything turned out so completely *right*. Almost always in the past, when he had finished something, unless it was a jigsaw-type thing that was either right or wrong, Dan had been left with the feeling that while it was very good indeed for his age, an older person would have done it better. It didn't matter how much his parents praised it – he *knew*. This time was different. This time you couldn't tell that he was only ten. You couldn't tell that it hadn't been done by a grown-up. And this on the very same day that he had completely confounded Lizzie with the Fish envelope trick! For once, this wasn't entirely coincidence. Dan, in the past hour, had felt a brand new surge of confidence buzzing through him. He had felt as if he could do *anything*. And this buzz, which made him sparkle and glow inside, was the thing that made it possible for him to look at the Spitfire through new eyes, and realise that there was absolutely nothing more he needed to do to it. It was *done*.

He laid the Spitfire gently down on the kitchen table.

And then it happened.

Max, who hadn't been looking at Dan, who had had no idea that there was anything to see other than his brother (who was in a bad mood with him) coming into the room, only noticed the flash of movement, and the sudden appearance of something or other on the table in the exact spot where Roger Dumpling was sitting. By instinct, without even thinking about it, he flung his arm outwards in a protective movement, and said, 'Mind Roger!'

The Spitfire flew off the table in a sideways direction, ricocheted off the freezer door, and crash-landed on the tiled kitchen floor, splintering into a dozen or more fragments.

Dan screamed.

Mrs Sharp whirled round. 'What . . . ?'

Max sat frozen in bewildered terror. He didn't understand what he'd done. The shattered pieces coming to rest on the floor looked nothing whatsoever like the beautiful aircraft he'd only just seen in Dan's room.

Dan had never been known to lose his temper. Nobody even knew that he had a temper. But all at once he exploded, launching himself at Max's neck with his hands ready in the strangling position. Max let out a scream of fright. His chair tipped backwards, hitting his mother, who caught it, more by accident than by skill.

Mr Sharp, who had heard two bloodcurdling screams

from two of his children in a matter of seconds, raced in from the garden with a chicken leg in his hand. Lizzie, watching the whole scene without being actually physically involved, thought later that he looked for all the world as if he were ready to protect his family with nothing but the chicken for a weapon (which was probably a bit unrealistic but nonetheless terribly brave).

He dropped the chicken, ran over and grabbed hold of Dan's arms. It took the combined efforts of both parents to wrestle him away from his brother before he could do any permanent damage.

'I didn't mean it!' Max sobbed.

'What happened? What's all this about? Dan, leave your brother alone and tell me what happened!'

'He broke my Spitfire!' shouted Dan. 'I'd just this minute finished it and nobody else had even seen it and he just knocked it off the table because he said that stupid Roger Dumpling was there! I'm sick of Roger Dumpling! I'm sick of Max!' He made another lunge towards Max, who wailed even louder. Mrs Sharp picked him up and held him at a safe distance.

Bonnie the three-quarters golden retriever picked up the chicken leg and slipped silently out into the garden.

It took at least a quarter of an hour to calm Dan down.

'Remember he's only seven!' said his mother.

'It was an accident!' said his father.

'It was not an accident! He did it on purpose!'

They offered him a brand new model kit. He could

have it first thing tomorrow. They'd drive into town and he could choose anything he wanted.

'I don't ever want to make a model again. There's no point doing anything in this house! It just gets ruined!'

Max, gulping back tears and his nose all runny, said he was sorry. Dan refused to look at him.

'He ought to be punished!'

'You know we never punish you for accidents,' said his father.

'It was not an accident!'

Round and round the conversation went. It might have gone on a good while longer, had it not been for the burning smell wafting in from the garden. Mr Sharp, looking suddenly stricken, rushed outside to find an entire family pack of chicken pieces scorched to cinders on the barbecue, while Bonnie gnawed away at the sole survivor in a distant corner of the garden, looking sheepish.

This latest disaster did at least go some way to breaking the mood. Dan muttered a few words of forgiveness to his brother, though he still couldn't quite manage to look at him. His father took him out for a drive, and the two of them picked up fish and chips in the village and brought them back for a replacement tea. The atmosphere remained distinctly subdued, but it seemed that the incident was over.

However, if they thought Dan was going to forget about it, they were wrong. Very wrong indeed.

13

Virtual Dalek Planet

Entering competitions was turning out to be rather more time-consuming than Lizzie had expected. She found another five prize contests in the weekend papers and four more in the satellite TV magazine. The postage would have ruined her, had it not been for an unexpected stroke of very good fortune.

Mr Sharp used the post a great deal, despite having e-mail and a fax available. Big brown envelopes usually. When Lizzie peeked round his office door and asked if she could borrow a few stamps, her father, who was sitting staring gloomily at the computer screen, just waved vaguely towards a drawer and said, 'Help yourself.' Lizzie could tell that the conversation hadn't really registered and that in a few minutes he would have forgotten all about it. She opened the drawer and found sheets of stamps, floating around in a messy sea of paper clips and elastic bands. Nobody could possibly need so many stamps. She tore off about thirty second-class ones and retreated rapidly. Her father didn't even look round.

Most of the magazines Lizzie had bought let you put all of your competition entries for one issue in the same envelope, so the stamps ought to last her a while. Also, she couldn't actually *do* all the competitions, because she didn't know all the answers. Like: 'Name the actor who played the first Doctor Who'. How was she supposed to know that? Even her parents didn't know. All they could come up with, after some consideration and conferring, was 'it definitely wasn't Jon Pertwee', which was not helpful. Lizzie could have made lengthy lists of people it definitely wasn't, all by herself.

The competitions were taking on a new significance in view of the continued absence of all the CDs. Lizzie had read out her wishlist again, in case the frequencies or the soundwaves or the astral lines, or whatever wishes were transmitted on, had all been busy the first time, and the wish hadn't got through. But still nothing. Although she didn't like to admit it even to herself, she was no longer entirely confident. There had been nothing since the duvet. And even the duvet... Lizzie had noticed, to her considerable discomfort, that there was a large and very new-looking Westalls department store carrier bag right at the top of the carrier bag drawer in the kitchen. She had a bad feeling about this. A small part of her was beginning to think that it was just as well she was sending all these competition entries in, because until she actually won a few of them nothing would turn up at all.

She sighed deeply, turned the page of *Wicked!* magazine and set about writing her entry for the Bonanza Cinema Ticket Giveaway (Qu: Who played the title role in the film *Evita*?).

There was a tap on the door.

'Go away,' said Lizzie.

The door opened, and: 'Thanks a lot,' said Dan, walking in.

Lizzie eyed him with disfavour. Dealings amongst the Sharp children had been distinctly cool of late. Dan was just about speaking to Max, but no more often than he could help. Max had been creeping around in a dejected sort of way, slinking off silently, presumably in the company of those wretched Dumplings. And she herself had by no means forgiven Dan for the whole Fish Envelope Episode, which she still did not understand, and which she felt had seriously tarnished her magical persona.

'I need your help,' said Dan.

Lizzie gave him a withering sort of look which said, more or less, 'You'll be lucky, matey.'

'Come on,' said Dan. 'You can't hold a grudge for ever.'

Lizzie gave him a look which said 'Try me and see.'

'It's in your own best interests,' said Dan.

Lizzie snorted. 'You don't seriously imagine for one second that I'll ever do anything to help you again in your entire life, unless you tell me how you cheated.' Lizzie had driven herself half crazy trying to work it out. It was the *detail* that was so confounding. Twins. Nothing had been said about twins when her school had been told at Assembly. Just 'Mrs Clarkson is leaving to have a baby'. She didn't doubt that there would turn out to be two babies. Dan knew what he was talking about. You could tell. But if nobody at her school had passed information to him, that ruled out every single suspect she could think of. Not many possible explanations remained.

Psychic powers (out of the question). Some kind of

article in the local paper – but why? *Double Whammy Baby Sensation at Cross Keys School! Or: Local Teacher Ditches Career in Multiple Birth Drama!* It didn't seem likely.

Some sort of private connection between her family and Fish? How could that happen without Lizzie knowing? She'd sounded out both her parents on the subject, but they had only met Fish for five minutes at a Parents' Evening and could barely even remember what she looked like.

'Why is it,' said Dan, 'that when I do something nobody can explain it's called cheating, and when you do something nobody can explain, it's magic?' Lizzie said nothing. 'Anyway, the thing is this. It's time to get rid of the Dumplings. I have had *enough* of the Dumplings. What happened on Friday' – he couldn't bear to go into any more detail – 'was the absolute final limit.'

Lizzie was interested despite herself.

'How can anybody possibly get rid of the Dumplings? They only exist in Max's head.'

'So that's where we have to get rid of them from,' said Dan. 'And you're the person to do it. What with the magic and all.'

Lizzie looked blank. It sounded as if she was being asked to perform an exorcism, which was a bit of of a heavy thing to ask of a young witch. And in any case, wasn't exorcism something you did to demons and devils and evil spirits? The Dumplings were an incredible nuisance, but she had never considered them to be instruments of Satan. And Dan didn't believe in magic anyway. Did he?

'You mix a potion,' said Dan patiently. 'A *Dumpling* potion. You boil it up and you sprinkle it all round the house and *kapow*! that will be that. No more Dumplings ever. Everyone you do potions on disappears and so will they. We'll have a nice normal household where you can't be yelled at for sitting on imaginary people. The *end*.'

'But,' said Lizzie. 'How can that possibly work? I can't do a spell on people that don't even exist. And you don't even believe in magic!'

'That's not the point,' said Dan. 'It doesn't matter what I believe. What matters is what Max believes. And Max believes that you can banish people with potions.'

Light began to dawn. 'So – what you're saying is – that Max believing in the potion would make it work? That next morning he'd wake up and *pffft*! the Dumplings would all be gone?'

'That's exactly what I'm saying. And it would be the best possible thing. Max is far too old to have these pretend friends. He needs a bit of help to let go of them. It would be doing him a *favour*. He gets teased and picked on at school the whole time, and it's not surprising, is it?'

'And of course none of this has anything to do with you wanting revenge for what happened to your aeroplane.'

Dan winced. 'All right,' he said. 'It's that as well. Just imagine if it had been you.'

'I don't make aeroplanes.'

'You know what I mean. Imagine if you'd just bought a brand new CD and left it by your bedroom window and Hercules Dumpling knocked it out and it fell in the barbecue and got roasted. You'd have flipped. You'd have thought just the same things I've been thinking. You'd probably have mixed the potion already.'

Lizzie had to allow that this was true. 'But all the same. It would really be cruel. The Dumplings are just about the only friends he's got.'

'Maybe they're the reason he doesn't have any other friends. Maybe he doesn't even try to make proper friends because he's got them. And maybe, like I said, other kids get put off because he's so *weird*. And think how gruesome it is when you have your own friends round and there's Max muttering away in the corner to somebody who isn't even there.'

It did, actually, make a lot of sense. Tara Bywater, on her first visit to Lizzie's house, had asked her, 'Does your little brother have to go to a special school?' which was really very worrying indeed.

'It's your chance to do something *good*!' Dan added, sensing that Lizzie was weakening.

Lizzie frowned. It had always been her intention to be a good witch. But, whichever way you looked at it, her record of goodness so far was not impressive. She'd broken a few bones, induced a nasty attack of projectile vomiting and made a long list of wishes, all of which had been for material goods entirely for her own pleasure. It had already occurred to her in passing that she should, perhaps, have made some rather more unselfish wishes. She could so easily have included a wish for world peace, or a wish that her father's next book would become a best seller. Although neither of these things, if they came to pass, would exactly do her any harm. Perhaps she should find something to wish for that would benefit somebody else and be no use to her at all. Perhaps she should wish for Max to make some friends?

'So you'll do it?' said Dan.

'I don't know.'

'Well. I could always do it myself. It would probably work.'

'*What*?'

'Max thinks magic runs in families,' said Dan. 'It wouldn't be hard to convince him that I can do it as well. All I'd have to do would be to look really confident.'

Lizzie didn't like the sound of this at all. Dan had undermined her magical powers quite enough lately without taking over the spellcasting. Perhaps she would do it. She did *enjoy* mixing potions and casting spells. But all the same, it was a bit much for Dan to be marching in here asking *her* for favours. It ought by rights to be the other way around.

'I'll do you a favour in return,' said Dan. Lizzie blinked. It was almost as if he had read her mind.

'What could you possibly do for me?'

'Well,' said Dan, 'I could tell you who the first Doctor Who was, for a start.'

'How did you know about that?'

'Mum and Dad keep talking about it. They've just decided it definitely wasn't somebody called Patrick Something. And Dad keeps wandering round going "Exterminate! Exterminate!" It's really embarrassing.'

Lizzie hesitated. The first prize for the Doctor Who competition was a video recorder – one of the things she most wanted.

'Do you really know the answer?'

'No. But I could find out in two minutes.'

'Yeah? Like how?'

'Look it up on the Internet,' said Dan. 'You can find out absolutely anything you want to know on the Internet. It's dead easy.'

Lizzie looked at him. 'Show me. Prove it.'

'So we have a deal then?'

'Well.' Lizzie picked up her magazines and flicked rapidly through them. 'There are actually five or six things I need to find out for these competitions. If you can get me all the answers I'll do the spell.'

'Excellent,' said Dan. 'Just give me the list.'

'Hang on. You could make up any old stuff and pretend it was the right answers. You have to show me that you can really do it.'

'You mean, you want to come into my *room*?'

'There's nothing really valuable left to damage,' said Lizzie, unkindly. 'Come along. I want to see this for myself.'

Dan shepherded Lizzie into his bedroom with great care. He tried to steer her straight to a chair by the computer out of harm's way, but she kept wanting to stop and look at things.

'What's *that*?'

'It's a map of Triangula.'

'Where?'

'You wouldn't be interested,' said Dan, moving the map out of harm's way. Dan loved to draw maps, and computer games gave him many opportunities. He spent hours and hours meticulously mapping games with beautiful neat fine-tipped felt pens. He had blocks of plain paper and squared paper in sizes A3 and A4. Sometimes drawing the map gave him more pleasure than the game ever did.

'And what's *that*?'

'Just a robot I'm building. Look, sit *down*.'

Lizzie sat. On the computer screen a three-dimensional pipe system was being created. Pale green pipes looped and turned in and out and up and down. Even as Lizzie watched a pink pipe and an orange pipe appeared simultaneously out of nowhere and began to coil and weave themselves around the green ones in a pastel rainbow of plumbing.

'What's that? Did you make it?'

'Don't be daft,' said Dan. 'It's a screensaver. Don't you know anything about computers?'

Lizzie knew more or less what a screensaver was but she'd never seen this one before. It was fascinating. All the pipes crumbled and disappeared; there was a moment's stillness and then a purple pipe appeared and it all started again.

Dan wiggled the mouse and the pipes vanished. He clicked a few things on the screen, and the computer came to life in a whirring of beeps and buzzes and clicks.

'What's all that? What's happening?'

'It's dialling. There's a modem inside the computer. You're amazing sometimes. I mean, don't you have computers at school?'

'Of course we do,' said Lizzie. 'But I've never been on the Internet. I think you can, if you go to Computer Club or something.'

'You have a Computer Club and you don't go?'

'Why would I go? It's all boys. Would you go to a club that was all girls?'

Dan shrugged; he supposed not. 'There we are,' he said. 'We're in.' *You have mail*, crooned a voice.

'You get *mail*?'

'It'll be from Brandon,' said Dan.

'Brandon?'

'He's a friend of mine. He's thirteen and he lives in Chicago. He plays all the same games as I do. We send each other save files and cheats.'

Lizzie blinked. 'But I've never even heard of him!' It seemed that her brother had a whole secret life of which she knew nothing. A friend in America! The sheer glamour of it. She began to wonder whether she had maybe been a bit hasty in turning down the computer when it had been offered to her.

'Anyway,' said Dan, who had no intention of letting Lizzie anywhere near Brandon. 'Here we go. Watch.' He typed 'Doctor Who' into a little box on the screen and pressed a button called Search. There was a brief pause and then: '436 Web Sites Found!' the computer announced triumphantly.

'Four hundred and thirty-*six*? Are you sure you've done it right?'

'Of course,' said Dan. 'There are web sites for absolutely everything. Things like Doctor Who that are sort of cult things always have hundreds and hundreds. Just look.'

He scrolled down the list. Doctor Who Quotes (insightful and ironic). The Cross-Referenced TimeLine Home Site. Doctor Who Fanclub Lists. Doctor Who Cuttings Archive, Doctor Who Chronology, Doctor Who Books Online. Virtual Dalek Planet. The Official Home Page of the Doctor Who Appreciation Society. The Tardis Databanks. Episode Guide. Doctor Who Simulation Sounds Page. Doom 2 Levels with a Doctor Who Theme. It was absolutely amazing.

'View Next 20 Matches?' the computer purred seductively.

'Minnesota Doctor Who Viewing Society,' read Lizzie. This struck her as unbearably funny. Minnesota must be a really desperate place.

'This will do,' said Dan, clicking on one of the listed websites. A new page appeared. 'This is the contents page. See that: "The Doctors"? That's what we want.' He clicked again and details of all the Doctor Whos since the beginning of time flashed up on the screen.

'There's your answer,' said Dan. 'William Hartnell,

Doctor Who 1963–1966. Told you it wouldn't take more than two minutes to find. And there's that Patrick, as well, the one it wasn't. And all the other ones it wasn't. Better tell Mum and Dad, it might calm them down a bit.'

'This is very good,' said Lizzie, reluctantly impressed. 'OK. I believe you. I'll give you a list of all the other questions I need answers to, just as soon as I've filled in the Doctor Who competition entry. It's due in by Saturday, and I *really* want the prize.'

'Fine,' said Dan. He actually enjoyed finding things out on the Internet. It was tremendously satisfying tracking down a nugget of information, and you often came across all sorts of weird and wonderful sites along the way, entirely by chance. But Lizzie was supposed to think he was doing her an enormous favour, so he didn't say that. 'And you'll do the Dumpling spell?'

'OK. Just as soon as I get the opportunity.'

'In the meantime,' said Dan, 'you'd better start thinking about what to use for the U in Dumpling. I've been thinking about it myself and I promise you it's not easy. But you're a witch! I know you'll come up with something.'

143

14

Bloaty Head

It took less time for Dan to find the answers to all Lizzie's competition questions than it had taken Lizzie herself to write them down for him. She was very taken by the Internet, and immediately added a computer to the list of things she wanted. She particularly liked the idea of making online friends in faraway places. She was sure that if she had access to the Internet she would make friends in places like California and Hawaii straightaway, and they would invite her to stay. Tatiana Belinsky began to seem very dull in comparison with such a prospect.

And all that information! Being able to find out absolutely anything! It crossed her mind that maybe – she couldn't quite see how, but then she hardly knew anything about it yet – maybe Dan had somehow used the Internet to find out about Fish and the twin baby Fish. Maybe Fish had her very own website, called Bitchbag.com or something. How could you tell?

Unfortunately none of the competitions she had so far found offered a computer as a prize. She made a mental note to buy some computer magazines. If only magazines weren't so expensive! Maybe they kept magazines in the library in Stonebridge. She could go in and write down all the competition details and it wouldn't cost her a penny. But transport in and out of

Stonebridge was so very difficult. Even if she got the bus, it needed her parents to drive her to and from the bus stop, and since they were too mean and cruel to let her have a mobile phone, how could she let them know when she was back and needing to be collected?

The mixing of the Dumpling Potion had to wait until the following Sunday, when Lizzie arrived back at lunchtime from spending Friday and Saturday night staying with her friend Natasha. Fortunately, during the afternoon Mr and Mrs Sharp decided to take the dog out for a long walk. All the children were invited to go with them, and for a worrying few moments there was a serious danger that Max, who didn't know that there was brewing planned, would accept. But Max said that his legs were a bit achy and they didn't feel like a long walk just at that moment.

Their father was disappointed. 'What's the matter with you all?'

'It's too hot,' said Lizzie. 'My head gets all bloaty if I walk in the heat.'

'It's a beautiful day,' said their father. 'What about you, Dan? Stretch those legs in the fresh air?'

'My legs are stretched already,' said Dan. 'I've been growing a lot lately. It's used up all my energy.'

'Achy legs! Bloaty head! *Growing*! I never heard such feeble excuses.'

Mrs Sharp made a 'young people nowadays!' sort of sound, and they set off, with a wildly excited Bonnie, who thought a long walk was just about the best thing in the world.

'At last!' said Dan, as the door closed behind them.

'The witching hour has arrived!' Lizzie opened the pots and pans cupboard, took out her cauldron and placed it on the cooker.

'There's going to be a potion?' Max looked up in surprise. 'Who's it going to be for?'

'Um.' Lizzie felt a twinge of discomfort. It wasn't really kind, to brew up a Dumpling potion while Max sat there all agog and asking if he could be her assistant and do an ingredient. But she had promised.

'Never mind,' said Dan. 'Watch the ingredients and see if you can work it out.' He and Lizzie had discussed the ingredients in some detail already. The problem of the U had not been easy to resolve. There was practically nothing edible or drinkable or pourable that began with a U.

'We'll have to combine it with some other letter,' he had said to Lizzie. 'Like you did with rabbit droppings.'

'Dumpling,' said Lizzie. 'U-M. Unripe mango.'

'We can't use unripe anything,' said Dan. 'If it's unripe it's waiting to be eaten. It would be *missed*. It's mouldy old stuff we can use.'

'D-U,' said Lizzie. 'Dad's umbrella.'

Dan snorted.

'Well! It's very difficult! Words just don't begin with U!'

'Diamond Ukelele!' said Dan, helpfully. 'Darkest Uruguay! Dirty Underwear!'

Lizzie threw a cushion at him.

'Donkey's Udders!' spluttered Dan. 'Dog's . . . oh!'

'Dog's what?'

'I just had a thought. I mean, if you can have rabbit droppings. Can't you work it out?'

'Dog's . . . *oh*! I see what you mean! But we can't!'

'Of course we can,' said Dan. 'Use your tiny brain.'

And so here they were.

'First the lemonade!' sang Lizzie, sloshing a generous amount from a two-litre bottle into the cauldron. In this sort of weather its disappearance would seem entirely natural. 'And ice!' She pulled an ice tray from the freezer and cracked out four or five cubes.

Max fetched a piece of paper and a pencil and wrote down 'L, I'. He wasn't much good at puzzles like this but he was prepared to give it his best shot.

'And now – some mashed potato!' Lizzie got out a packet of ready-mix potato granules, and sprinkled a portion into the brew, which was starting to bubble gently already. She wasn't at all sure of the effect of mixing them with lemonade rather than water, but thought on the whole that it wouldn't make a great deal of difference other than that the potato would be fizzier. Which would probably improve it. Almost all drinks were nicer if they were fizzy, so why not food as well?

Max wrote down M and P.

'Flavourings!' said Lizzie, sprinkling nutmeg and ginger into the softly frothing mixture, and stirring it vigorously. A warm spicy aroma began to float into the room; this potion actually smelled rather delicious. Perhaps, entirely by chance, she'd stumbled on the recipe for a never-before-tried pudding, which would take the world by storm. She would call it Sweet Spicy Dumplings. The bubbling blobs of fizzy potato did, totally by coincidence, have a sort of dumplinglike appearance. Perhaps she could construct an entire book of recipes with ingredients whose first letters spelled their name, and see if anybody noticed.

Except, of course, that there was one ingredient left to add, and it was most certainly not something you could include in a recipe book.

'And now,' she announced dramatically, 'it is time for the Final Ingredient!'

'Can I do it please?' asked Max, as she had somehow known he would. 'You've always let me before.'

'I'm afraid that on this occasion that won't be possible.' said Lizzie. 'This ingredient is famously hard to obtain. You have to get up at the crack of dawn and silently stalk your prey in the hope of being able to get some of this very special liquid. Only the most dedicated witch is capable of creating potions which require it.'

Max couldn't imagine Lizzie getting up at the crack of dawn for anything. 'What is it? Did you get some already?'

'I am very devoted to my art,' said Lizzie. 'And by creeping out at sunrise and waiting with infinite patience, I have indeed obtained a supply of the ingredient. Wait here while I fetch it.'

'I'll take over the stirring,' said Dan.

Max looked at the letters he'd written down. L, I, M, P, N, G. Limping? Was this a limping spell and not the name of a person at all? What use would that be? Could

Lizzie perhaps be mixing a potion to make herself limp so she could get out of games on Monday? This didn't seem unlikely.

'Why aren't you doing it?' he asked Dan.

'Doing what?'

'The letters. Working out what they spell.'

'I already know,' said Dan, continuing to stir and not looking round.

'You *know*?' Max's spirits, which hadn't been high in the first place, took a sudden *thud*. Lizzie had told Dan, the famous non-believer, about this potion, and she hadn't told Max, who had always been her loyal follower and assistant? What was going on?

Lizzie returned with a small glass containing about two inches of a yellowy liquid. She didn't notice Max looking at her in an extremely hurt way.

'The final ingredient!' she said. 'Dog's urine!'

'*What*?'

'Dog's urine,' said Lizzie, tipping the liquid into the cauldron and taking the wooden spoon back from Dan.

'Urine? Isn't that – pee?'

'Exactly so.'

Max was gobsmacked. 'You mean – you went and got that from Bonnie – in that little glass – while she was ...' This was disgusting. It was much, much worse than the rabbit droppings, though he wasn't quite sure why.

'I used a large pot,' said Lizzie. 'And it was *not* fun. This is the downside of being a witch. Collecting the nastier ingredients.' None of this was true. The fluid in the glass was in fact dry white wine, taken from a bottle of New Zealand Chardonnay which their mother had fortunately opened the day before. As Dan had pointed out, since this wasn't a real spell it didn't matter *what* it was. All that mattered was what Max *believed* it was. Lizzie had seen the sense in this, though she had taken the trouble to check that she wouldn't be casting a spell on somebody by accident. The letters WMPLING could not possibly be arranged into any kind of a word, so it seemed safe enough.

Max continued to look absolutely astounded.

'I think this is ready,' said Lizzie. She removed the potion from the heat and poured it carefully into an empty milk bottle. It was a thicker, creamier potion than the previous ones, no doubt on account of the mashed potato. The wine had if anything improved the smell.

'But what *is* it?' asked Max, looking in bewilderment at the letters he'd written down, which now read: LIMPNGDU. Max couldn't do that trick Dan did, re-arranging the letters in his head. He wasn't a good enough reader.

There was a long silence. 'What *is* it?' he asked again, suddenly uneasy. 'And why does Dan know it already? What's going on?'

'Let's just do the Circle of Doom,' Dan said. 'Then we'll tell you all about it.'

'But I don't *want* to do the Circle of Doom,' Max said. There was something terribly wrong here. *Dan* prattling away about Circles of Doom was not the way things ought to be.

'Perhaps we should tell him,' said Lizzie, after a

moment. 'Perhaps we should think about this.'

'I'll do it myself, then,' said Dan, and he snatched up the vial and disappeared.

Max looked at Lizzie, who avoided his gaze.

'What's going *on*?'

'Wait till Dan gets back,' Lizzie said gruffly. She was starting to feel quite wretched about all of this. What had they done? How had she let Dan talk her into it? Well, it was his idea and he could flipping well be the one to tell Max.

Dan returned, the vial empty. 'All done,' he said. 'Sprinkled to the North, the South, the East and the West.'

Nobody said anything.

'I think you'd better tell him what it was,' Lizzie said eventually.

Dan went over and looked at the letters Max had written.

'You got all the letters right,' he said. 'Can't you see what the word is?' Dan had the sort of brain that arranges letters into anagrams very easily.

Max didn't speak.

'Look,' said Dan. 'I'll show you.' He took the pencil and, one by one, crossed the letters out, writing each crossed-out letter underneath so they formed a new order.

DUMPLING, they said.

Max gave a tiny ouch-like sound and seemed visibly to shrink. He didn't lift his eyes from the paper.

'Hey, Max,' said Lizzie, suddenly stricken. 'Don't look like that. It was only a joke.'

151

Max didn't look at her.

'The potions never work until the next day,' Dan said cheerfully. 'You've got all evening to say goodbye.'

It would have been better, they thought later, if Max had got angry with them. If he'd shouted at them that they were mean and cruel, that they were horrible people. If he'd said anything at all. But he just sat there a few moments longer in total silence, before pushing back his chair, running out of the kitchen without a backward glance at them, and slamming the door behind him.

'Oh, Dan,' said Lizzie. 'What have we done?'

15

L is for Lager

Most certainly, they should not have done it.

Never had Lizzie thought she would wish so desperately for a spell not to work. But of course it did. It was just exactly as Dan had said. Max's belief in Lizzie's powers was absolute, and the next day when he awoke the Dumplings were not there. And without them Max was bereft. They were his best friends. Lizzie and Dan never had time for him. And – this was somehow the worst thing – because Max trusted in Lizzie so deeply, because he had such staunch and unmovable faith in her powers, his best friends had left him forever.

Lizzie couldn't bear it. She tried talking to him.

'It was just a joke, Max. It wasn't a proper spell.'

Max looked at her blankly. All the life seemed to have been drained out of him. 'Of course it was a proper spell,' he said. 'It worked, didn't it?'

'But only because you *thought* it was a proper spell. And now I'm telling you that it wasn't. I can only do magic on real people, Max. The Dumplings were real to you but they were way outside my powers. The Dumplings are your *own* magic. You were the person who made them exist in the first place and only you could make them go away.'

Max just shrugged. He had nothing to say to her. He

drifted around the house in a silent little bubble of unhappiness. He sat staring aimlessly out of windows. He began to bite his nails.

Lizzie was distraught. Her magic had never been intended for anything like this. She felt unfit to be a witch. She would have done anything to make things better. She cancelled every single one of her wishes for CDs and videos and computers and asked that they all be exchanged for either (a) the Dumplings to be brought back or (b) even better, some real friends for Max. He had always been a good little brother. All his life he had followed her around and wanted to be with her and wanted her to play with him; he'd believed in her magic and been her loyal and faithful assistant. How *could* she have done this?

Dan, meanwhile, was feeling even worse, but had no way to show it. He knew all too well that all the reasons he had given for getting rid of the Dumplings for Max's own good had just been invented to persuade Lizzie. The plain and simple truth was that he had wanted revenge. At the time, the destruction of his Spitfire had felt like the worst thing that had ever happened to him. Even after he had pretended to forgive Max, the anger burned away inside him furiously. It destroyed his peace of mind. He couldn't concentrate on things. He would sit at the computer designing satellite towns for his *Metropolis* city Triangula, a process which usually absorbed his entire concentration, but all he could see was the shattered aircraft and the total unfairness of everything. If he could pay Max back, he thought, the pain would be cancelled out; it would go away and he

154

could get on with the rest of his life in peace.

But of course it hadn't worked out like that at all. It should all have been so simple, like a fight in a computer game. Dan had taken considerable damage. He had launched a counter-attack, which would also inflict considerable damage. And so everything became equal again. It was all cancelled out.

Except that was how it worked in computer games. This was real life, and Dan could tell already that it was entirely different. He, Dan, had lost a model aircraft. It had taken ages and ages to build, and nobody had ever seen it finished, and the pain when it was so needlessly ruined had been excruciating. But ten days had passed since then. His fury had faded and he could now see that the damage need not be permanent. The first time he'd built the Spitfire it had taken nearly four months. But his parents had offered to buy him a replacement kit – or any other kit – and he knew, if he was honest about it, that he had learned so much from his mistakes the first time that he could build another one in probably less than three weeks, And it would be *better* than the first one, because he would know where he had gone wrong the first time and been forced to cover up mistakes which he would not make again.

Max meanwhile had lost his best friends, who could not be replaced by driving into Stonebridge and buying a new kit from the model shop. They were gone forever. And it was all Dan's fault.

Dan began, all too late, to realise how *useful* the Dumplings had been. Whenever you wanted to go off and do something on your own, the Dumplings arrived to entertain Max and set you free. Now Max wafted around like a lost soul and the very sight of him was like a knife through Dan's heart.

He tried to make it up to Max by playing with him, even though Max was so awfully bad at games. He offered to play Man Utd v Chelsea, which in normal times Max would have been thrilled at. But:

'No, thanks,' said Max, distantly.

'What?'

'Can't be bothered,' said Max, and wandered off upstairs to his room, where he was spending more and more time, frequently being overheard having long, one-sided conversations with his hamster, Zippy.

Dan was stunned. His own little brother disliked him so much he didn't want to play football with him. And he was perfectly right. Dan had been mean and spiteful and vengeful and all things horrible. And he could find no way to make amends.

He went up and knocked on Lizzie's door.

'We have to do something,' he said abruptly.

There was no need for Lizzie to ask what he meant.

'Well,' she said sharply. 'Have you got any bright ideas? I've thought and thought about it. I don't know yet how to do the spell to make people come back. I can only make them go away. Max knows that.'

'Couldn't you pretend? Mix up the same ingredients and do something completely different with it?'

Lizzie's heart sank at the thought of making another Dumpling potion. 'He wouldn't believe me,' she said.

Two weeks ago she would have been confident that her little brother trusted her so completely that he would have believed anything. He had no reason to trust her any more. 'He's not stupid.'

'There must be something you can do,' Dan persisted.

'Why *me*?'

'Because you're the one he thinks is a witch. Perhaps if you did one more spell. Cast a spell on somebody he *wants* to get rid of.'

'Get rid of? He hasn't *got* anybody. That's the problem!'

'I'm sure he said ages ago that there was someone he wanted a spell cast on. Why not ask him? What have we got to lose?'

'I'll ask him,' said Lizzie.

'Nathan Dursley,' said Max.

At least he was speaking to them. He didn't look as if he was enjoying it much, but he was speaking to them. Ten days of being treated as if they were invisible had thoroughly unnerved Dan and Lizzie.

'Oh, I remember now,' said Lizzie. 'Rachel Dursley's little brother.'

'Jacob and Ben Dursley's little brother,' said Dan.

'Would you like me to cast a spell on him, Max?' Lizzie asked.

'I asked you that before,' said Max. 'You wouldn't. You said he was just a little boy and it might go wrong and you might change him into a road.'

A whole proper-length sentence!

'That was a long time ago,' said Lizzie. 'I'm much more experienced now. I'm sure it will be absolutely fine.'

Max looked at her. Lizzie felt herself shrivel inside at the ferocity of the stare.

'I'll have to do the Circle of Doom myself,' he said eventually. 'At school. You won't be there.'

'That won't be a problem,' Lizzie said encouragingly. 'You know exactly how it's done. Even *Dan* can do a Circle of Doom by now.' There was a long silence as everybody recalled the occasion on which Dan had done a Circle of Doom. Lizzie bit her lip.

'So shall I mix you a potion?' Lizzie asked, hopefully.

'I want dog's urine,' said Max.

'You what?'

'Dog's urine. In the potion. DU. Like the Dump... like the other spell. I want that.'

'Of course!' Lizzie said. 'It's a very powerful ingredient. It's very highly recommended.'

'I want to come with you when you collect it.'

'You can't want that, Max!' said Lizzie in horror.

'Why not?'

'Because it's not *fair*. On poor Bonnie. Think about it. She's a *girl*. It's not right to make her pee into a bowl in front of a boy.'

'She's a *dog*,' said Max.

'So you think she hasn't got feelings? Be reasonable. I'll have to get up at the crack of dawn – again! – and catch her off guard. She's absolutely desperate first thing in the morning because she's been indoors all night. It's the only time of day that it's *possible*. It's no good two of us going down. Mum or Dad would be bound to hear something. Just leave it to me. You can mix up all the ingredients together. And I promise you they'll be the absolute best ingredients ever. It will be ten times better than any other spell I've ever done. All right?'

'All right,' said Max. And for a brief moment Lizzie could almost have sworn she saw the shadow of a smile flash across his face. Maybe things would be all right after all.

Lizzie and Dan went together to check out the Drinks Cupboard. Dan wanted to be as involved in this spell as possible. He knew it probably wouldn't make any difference, and he most certainly didn't believe in magic, but on this occasion he felt a certain duty to show willing.

'If there isn't any white wine I don't know what we're going to do,' Lizzie said. 'There's nothing else that anybody could possibly mistake for dog's urine.'

Dan had already decided that he was never in his entire life going to drink white wine.

'There *isn't* any white wine,' he said. There were loads and loads of bottles of other stuff, but none looked anything like the right colour. There was rum, whisky, vodka, brandy, sherry, gin and port. There were things called Cointreau and Amaretto which he had never even heard of. He had never dreamed there was so much alcohol on the premises.

Lizzie peered at the bottles. 'This isn't the stuff they

drink,' she said. 'I think they keep this for guests. Look.' She ran a finger down the nearest bottle; the finger came up coated with dust. 'I don't think anybody's drunk this stuff for *years*.'

'You'll have to go and get some real dog's pee then,' said Dan. 'I expect it won't be so bad. It's just like you said. Catch Bonnie first thing in the morning with a large bowl and it'll probably be fine.'

Lizzie felt quite faint at the thought.

'Hang on,' she said.

'Yes?'

'This is what they *don't* drink. I know what they drink. Especially in the summer. Mum drinks white wine and Dad drinks lager. And both of those are things you keep in the fridge.'

They looked at each other for a moment, and then ran into the kitchen and threw open the fridge door.

Inside, there sat a brand new bottle of Chardonnay (about one-third gone) and a four-pack of lager cans, three of which remained.

'This is just absolutely perfect,' said Lizzie. 'We've caught them at exactly the right time. They won't notice. L is for lager. If you have a brand new pack of four you know it. If you have only one left you know it. If you only have two or three you are never going to be sure exactly which. We can take one with no problem at all. The brew will bubble and fizz and it'll work like a dream.'

'Yes, well,' said Dan, who was beginning to see complications. 'You haven't thought about this properly.

Nathan Dursley isn't somebody who only exists inside Max's head. He's real.'

'Oh, it won't do him too much damage,' Lizzie said airily. 'I doubt if we're talking anything more serious than a sprained ankle. And even if it's worse than that, he'll probably be glad of all the time off school. He'll get terribly spoiled and bought lots of presents. He ought to be *grateful*.'

'You're still not thinking properly,' said Dan. 'According to your rules, the spell won't work at all. You're not using the proper ingredients. You're using something beginning with W instead of something beginning DU.'

Lizzie paused. 'I suppose that's right,' she said uncertainly. 'This time, what Max *believes* it is won't make any difference.'

'And so nothing will happen to Nathan Dursley.'

'Something might happen to him anyway. Little boys are always having accidents.' It didn't sound very convincing. 'I tell you what,' she said. 'You know this kid, right?'

'I know who he is. I wouldn't say I know him. He's only seven.'

'Well, couldn't you sort of knock him over in the playground?'

'I can't do that!' Dan was horrified.

'Why not?'

'You're asking me to beat up a little kid!'

'I didn't say beat up. Just a little push or a trip will probably do fine. Nobody will ever believe you did it on purpose. You've not got a record of violence. Have you?'

'No,' said Dan. 'But I can't do it! What if he lands on his head and cuts it open and gets brain damage?'

'It won't happen,' said Lizzie. 'Little kids bounce. Come on, Dan. Don't you want to make it up to Max? I'm doing my bit. You're doing *nothing*.'

'Anyway,' said Dan, 'just supposing, for the sake of argument, that I did knock him over in the playground, which of course I'm not going to. What then? Kid gets taken away and sewn back together, everyone says it must have been an accident, Dan Sharp would never do such a thing on purpose. Though actually, now I come to think of it, if people know that Nathan Dursley bullies my little brother they'll probably think I *did* do it on purpose. Anyway, Max is going to *know* what happened. Quite probably he'll *be* there. He's hardly going to think it was magic.'

'Well, can't you get the kid on his own? In the toilets or something?'

This was going from bad to worse. 'Now you're asking me to mug a little kid in the toilets! I could get suspended!'

'I'm very disappointed in you,' said Lizzie. 'It really isn't much to ask. Oh well. Maybe if all the other ingredients are extra-good, it'll work anyway. I'm going to put loads and loads of alcohol in. It'll be wicked.'

16

Big, Big Trouble

Max trotted into school the next day with a secret smile, and with a bottle of extra-potent Dursley potion in his schoolbag. Apart from the dog's urine, it contained rum, sherry, and lager (lots!) together with a generous dollop of egg yolk. It had been very entertaining for Max, watching Lizzie and Dan put this lethal cocktail together for him. And Dan not even believing in magic! You had to laugh, you really did.

They had fussed and fidgeted and fumed together over getting the potion just perfect. Max had just sat there perched on a stool, kicking his legs and watching without comment. They argued away over the correct method to extract the yolk from an egg, wasting an entire egg in the process while Lizzie made flamboyant gestures which resulted in the yolk breaking and seeping disastrously into the white. Then Dan had a go, and managed to drain away all the white, which was actually a transparent sort of runny goo, through a crack in the shell, saving a perfectly rounded ball of yellow which went straight into the potion. It was wonderful to watch.

And all the alcohol! None of the other potions had been alcoholic. This one was practically explosive.

'How are you going to get this to school safely, Max?' fussed Lizzie.

'Use one of my drink bottles.' Max had a number of fun-size lemonade bottles with screw tops which he took to school.

Lizzie poured potion into a fun-size bottle. It foamed and bubbled like mad. The lager had proved to be a very exciting ingredient. Lizzie stopped, waited for the bubbling to subside and then very carefully topped it up.

'It won't all go,' she said. 'There was such a lot of lager.'

'That's fine.' said Max. 'Just put the rest of it in another bottle. You never know when I'll need it.'

'OK,' said Lizzie. She would have done absolutely anything he asked.

And so Max now had two bottles of violently active Dursley potion. One was in his bag; the second one he had buried under the hedge between their garden and Potters Field. He had dug quite a deep hole and he thought it would be safe enough. It was quite true that inside their house, nothing was safe from their mother. You just had to have the imagination to think of something better.

And now he could cast a spell on Nathan Dursley. It would be sheer magic.

'You bet it will,' said Tatiana Dumpling.

Max smiled.

The Dumplings, of course, had not really disappeared. Everything Lizzie said had been entirely true. Her magic could not possibly affect the Dumplings. They were entirely up to him. All that had changed was that the Dumplings had become secret. Nobody except Max would know about them any more.

There had been some other slight changes. Hercules Dumpling, who was altogether too loud a person to suit the Dumplings' new, quieter image, had, like many others before him, grown up and left. He had been replaced by a set of twins called Tatiana and Belinsky Dumpling. The twins were half Polish and half Ukrainian and they were very very clever. They were the sort of people you definitely wanted on your side.

Max hadn't set out to deceive his brother and sister. He had been fairly stunned that they would do such a monstrously cruel thing as to cast a spell on the Dumplings. He had needed quite a lot of quiet time out to himself to think about that. But while he was thinking, it had been impossible not to notice Lizzie and Dan tiptoeing about with anguished expressions, falling over themselves to be nice to him to make amends. He realised fairly quickly that it would be a serious mistake to let them know that the spell hadn't worked. And so he wandered around looking tragic, whispering silently inside his head to the Dumplings whenever he wanted to, and his brother and sister grew more and more miserable all the time.

And now he had two bottles of Dursley potion! It was *almost* time to forgive them. He'd just wait and see what the spell did, first.

Max had given much thought to the Circle of Doom. He could go right round the school building without attracting suspicion, but there were other Dursleys in the school: Ben Dursley in Dan's year and Jacob Dursley in Year Six. There was a real danger that the damage would happen to the wrong Dursley. This would be a great disappointment and a considerable waste, even though he had the second bottle in reserve.

So what he had in mind was to slip back into his own classroom while everyone else was outside at break, and sprinkle the potion around the table where Nathan sat with Robert Crane and Alex Matthews and Laurence Hunter. To the North, the South, the East and the West, completing an admittedly small but nonetheless perfect Circle of Doom. And then there could be no possible mistake. And if the spell took about one day to work, then with any luck it would happen either in class or during break tomorrow morning. Most probably during break – Nathan would be racing around in the playground like a mad thing as usual, and could very easily suffer a drastic injury. But either way, it was fine. Max would be there to watch.

The main difficulty was that it might rain, in which case everybody would stay indoors. It wasn't actually raining at present but it looked as if it was just about to. Even so, it would surely have stopped by lunchtime. He could do the spell just as easily then. If it rained all day – well, then he was going to have a problem.

The bell rang for the start of school; a few drops of rain began to spatter down. Max sighed. It would be a long, long morning.

As if to tease him, the rain stopped and started and stopped again. The funny thing was, his class were actually doing Weather as a topic this term, and every day they had to fill in a chart with little symbols like the ones they used when they did the weather on TV. Max normally enjoyed this very much: drawing little yellow suns and clouds, and diagonal lines to show rain, and checking the temperature. Once there had been a thunderstorm, and they'd had a fine time drawing dramatic zigzaggy lightning flashes. Today, however, looking at the chart just rubbed in the cruel fact that the previous nine schooldays had *all* been uninterrupted sunshine. How unlucky could you get?

Max stared absently across the room at Nathan Dursley, who caught the glance and fired back a deeply menacing stare. Normally Max would have buried his head in his work and pretended to be at the South Pole, but today was different. Today he had *power*, and he just stared back, undaunted. Nathan Dursley, without taking his eyes off Max for a single moment, leaned over and whispered something to Robert Crane. Robert Crane turned round and gazed at Max. Soon the whole table would have been staring at him, but at that moment Miss Parrish arrived there with a *swish* and demanded to know what was so interesting over there in the corner? and reluctantly they all looked back down at their weather charts.

Slowly, agonisingly slowly, the minutes ticked away. Ten minutes before the bell rang for break, a heavy flurry of rain blew against the window panes. That, it seemed, was that – the weather had finally made its decision. But then five minutes later, as if to say: 'Fooled you again!' the rain died away, the sky lightened and the sun broke through.

'Well, it looks as if you can go outside after all,' said Miss Parrish, peering through the window. 'Be careful, everyone, remember it's been raining and the ground may be slippery.'

There was a general stampede for the door. Max joined on towards the end, and loitered in the corridor outside, pretending to look at the collages pinned to the wall. There was a very slight danger that Miss Parrish would decide to stay in the classroom for break. Nearly always she went to the staff room for a cup of coffee, but sometimes when she had things to get ready she stayed behind. Max's nerves were beginning to feel somewhat strained – it would be awful to have to go through all this again tomorrow. And the day after that would be Friday, and it was out of the question to cast the spell on Friday and completely miss the results. So then he'd have to wait until next week, which was the last week of term. And after that he wouldn't get another chance until September! Max began, very faintly, to panic.

But it was all right. Just at that minute, Miss Parrish came out of the classroom, and, flashing a warm smile at Max, set off walking briskly in the opposite direction, tapping along on her clackety heels.

At last, his moment had arrived.

Max took the potion bottle out from his bag and slipped back into the classroom. He padded silently over to Nathan's table. He really ought to be quick. He wasn't supposed to be indoors, unsupervised.

It was not going to be possible to use up the entire potion. That would leave too much mess on the floor. But a few drops would be all right. After all the rain, Miss Parrish would hardly be surprised to see patches of wet here and there when the class trooped back in after break.

Max unscrewed the bottle, very very carefully, and sprinkled a few drops of potion behind where Nathan sat. Excellent! Now all he had to do was complete the Circle of Doom, and it would all be over, and he could just sit back and glow with pleasant anticipation, imagining all the dreadful possible fates that awaited Nathan Dursley next day. It would almost be a disappointment when one of them actually happened and he had to stop imagining the others.

He went around the table anti-clockwise, stopping once at each side to sprinkle potion. Abracadabra alaka*zam*!

'And what do you think *you're* doing?'

Max froze. His first, wild, thought was that Miss Parrish must have come back early and now he would be in all sorts of trouble. Then he realised it wasn't her voice that had spoken. It wasn't a grown-up voice at all.

Max wheeled round and looked straight into the eyes of Nathan Dursley.

'What're you doing in here?' Nathan said again. 'And what were you doing staring at me this morning? You're not allowed to stare at me. And what's that you've got in your hand?'

Max saw no reason to provide answers to any of these questions.

Nathan barged into him impatiently and grabbed the potion bottle.

'What've you got today then?' He sniffed the bottle suspiciously. 'It's a disgusting colour. What is it?'

'It's mine,' Max said mildly. 'You ought to give it back.'

Nathan laughed aloud, and took a large swig from the bottle. '*Bluuurgh*!' He coughed and spluttered. 'What *is* it? What's this?'

'It's probably a bit too strong for you,' said Max. He ought to be scared, he really knew he ought, but somehow it was not possible to watch your worst enemy drinking a liquid that contained dog's urine, and still have any room left over to feel fear. In fact, if anything Max felt calmer than he could ever remember feeling in his entire life. It was as if a completely new Max had emerged and taken over; a Max who stood serenely unpanicked, who could think of just exactly the right words to say, a Max who was in control of the situation. And it felt absolutely wonderful.

Nathan Dursley eyed him with scorn.

'What do you mean it's too strong for me?'

Max didn't bat an eyelid. 'What I said. It's too strong for you. I've said it twice now. Watch my lips when they move.' He remembered Dan saying these very words to Lizzie a couple of weeks ago – and as if by magic, they had lodged themselves in Max's memory and come tripping fluently off his tongue at exactly the right moment. 'I can drink it,' he went on. 'But you wouldn't be able to. Probably it would make you ill. You'd better give it back.'

Nathan looked at him uncertainly, his podgy little hand still firmly gripping the bottle. Max could almost read his mind. He was thinking: Obviously this useless little shrimpy gobslime Max Sharp can drink this stuff, or else why would it be in his drink bottle? And if he can drink it, then...

Nathan glared at Max, put the bottle into his mouth, tipped back his head and swallowed the lot. Then he sat down rather suddenly. The bottle fell out of his hands and rolled away across the floor. He looked at Max with an expression that was meant to be defiant, but which actually looked much more like somebody who is struggling with increasingly urgent waves of nausea.

'It wasn't *all* alcohol,' Max said encouragingly. 'Quite a lot of it was dog pee.'

Three things happened at once.

Miss Parrish arrived back in the classroom, looked at the boys with surprise and said, 'What are you two doing in here?'

The bell rang for the end of break.

And Nathan Dursley tipped over the edge of his chair and collapsed in a heap on the floor.

'What's wrong with Nathan?' Miss Parrish rushed over and knelt down on the floor by Nathan, inadvertently getting her skirt damp with the sprinkled potion. 'Nathan! Max, what happened to him?'

The rest of the class began to trickle back into the classroom in twos and threes, their chatter hushing abruptly as they realised there was a drama in progress.

'Bleeeeurgh,' said Nathan, apparently in his sleep. Stuff was starting to dribble out of the corner of his mouth.

'Nicole,' said Miss Parrish, picking out the most responsible of the girls, 'please go straightaway and fetch Mrs Allinson. Hurry!'

Nicole squeaked and raced out of the room. Mrs Allinson taught one of the Reception classes and was also the school's first-aid expert.

'Max, what happened?' Miss Parrish asked him again, more frantically this time. 'He just seemed to fall right off his chair. Had he been feeling ill? Is that why you were inside?'

'Actually, I think he's drunk,' said Max.

There followed a scene of great confusion. Mrs Allinson came rushing in, soon followed by the headmistress, Mrs Grieves; they both conferred with Miss Parrish and all three of them set about interrogating Max, whilst at the same time exchanging worried remarks about Nathan, who had by now been placed in the recovery position while everyone worked out what to do next. ('Do you think we should call an ambulance?' 'Should we try to make him sick?') Nothing like this had ever happened before. They all knew exactly what to do for the more everyday Year Two ailments: nosebleeds, scraped knees, banged elbows. None of them had ever previously had to deal with alcoholic stupor in a seven-year-old boy.

'Do you know exactly what he drank, Max?'

'Where did he get it from?'

'What *was* it? Max, it's very important that we know!'

Max realised that he was not yet even in trouble.

Nobody thought he was actually responsible. They just thought he'd been *there*. If he told them exactly what had been in the bottle all that would change straight-away. But if he *didn't* tell them, Nathan might die, and that was surely taking things a bit too far. And – if he was quite honest – there was quite a large part of him that *wanted* people to know that he was responsible. That Max Sharp was not somebody to be taken lightly. That you might tease or taunt or bully him, and think you were getting away with it for a while, but eventually, when you least expected it, he would, fearlessly and without regard for the consequences, extract the most terrible vengeance.

'Rum!' he said.

'R*um*?'

'Not just rum. Sherry. And lager!' He felt somehow unable to mention the dog's urine in front of three female teachers, all of whom were already looking at him in shock, horror and disbelief. But he would make sure all the other *children* heard about it. That wouldn't be difficult. It was the sort of thing which you only had to tell one other person and the whole class would know by lunchtime.

'*Bleeeeugh-glurggggh*!' All heads turned back to look at Nathan Dursley, who opened his eyes briefly, closed them again, opened his mouth and was spectacularly, violently, copiously sick. It seemed almost impossible that such a tremendous quantity of foul-smelling fluid could spurt out of the mouth of one small boy in a single gush. Miss Parrish and Mrs Allinson, both kneeling on the floor beside him, looked down, appalled, as their laps filled up with the contents of Nathan's last three meals, in various stages of digestion. There was a ripple of *oooohs!* and *aaaahs!* from the rest of the class, none of whom had ever seen anything like this in their lives before, or expected to ever again.

Mrs Grieves, the headmistress, put her hand firmly on Max's shoulder and swivelled him around until he was facing her.

'Max Sharp,' she said in tones of pure ice. 'I think you had better come along with me to my room and have a talk.'

The trouble was about to begin. Big, big trouble.

17

Life in the Liquor Den

They phoned Max's father at home and asked him to come in to school straightaway.

They also phoned Nathan's mother, who arrived and whisked Nathan off in the car. It had been decided, after Nathan was so very, very sick, that there couldn't really be enough of anything left inside him to do much harm, and so an ambulance had not after all been sent for, much to the disappointment of everyone watching.

Both Miss Parrish and Mrs Allinson had to go home and get themselves changed and cleaned up, which meant there were two classes with nobody to look after them. Miss Parrish's class didn't even have a classroom until after lunch; although the floor had been thoroughly cleaned and disinfected, the smell was still too awful for the room to be used straightaway.

All in all, the disruption to the school was considerable.

'Lager!' Mrs Grieves said to Max's father. 'Lager, and rum, and sherry!'

Mr Sharp's face was a curious mixture of relief, guilt and bewilderment. Relief, because clearly Max hadn't come to any harm. They'd told him that on the phone, but he hadn't quite believed it until he arrived and saw for himself. Guilt, because Mrs Grieves was eyeing him in such a way as to imply that any household which was so disreputably run that seven-year-old children were able to help themselves freely to such an unlikely mixture of alcoholic beverages, clearly left a great deal to be desired. And bewilderment – well, who wouldn't be bewildered? Why on earth would Max do such a thing?

'Max,' he said, turning his head away from the gimlet gaze of Mrs Grieves. 'Why on earth would you do such a thing?'

'And then to give all this alcohol to another child!' said Mrs Grieves. An innocent child, her tone implied. A child of pure habits, uncorrupted by life in the liquor den that was the Sharp home.

'You took this – this drink – to school and gave it to another child, Max?'

'I didn't *give* it to him,' said Max. 'He *took* it.'

Mrs Grieves looked disbelieving. 'Nathan Dursley just *took* your drink bottle?'

'*Ohhhh*,' said Mr Sharp. 'Of course! Now I see what's happened. I understand the whole thing.'

Max looked at him with some alarm. How could this be? His father didn't know the first thing about potions, spells and Circles of Doom. Or did he? It suddenly occurred to Max that if magic powers were indeed, as he hoped and suspected, inherited, then Lizzie must have inherited hers *from* someone. And if Max had to guess which of his parents was responsible, he would choose his dad, for sure. But even if his father did know what was going on, surely he would have the wit to realise that it wasn't the sort of thing you could possibly explain

176

to somebody like Mrs Grieves? If he started telling her stuff about Circles and Magic and Spells, the next thing to happen would be that a social worker would come round to their house and take all three of them into care.

Max tried urgently to signal the wisdom of silence to his father. But:

'It's all suddenly slotted into place,' said Mr Sharp.

'And are you going to be kind enough to explain it to me?' Mrs Grieves asked him.

'Of course,' said Mr Sharp.

Max hung his head in despair.

'The strange thing is, in a way I feel responsible,' said his father. 'I almost put him up to it!'

Mrs Grieves eyed Mr Sharp with, if such was possible, even greater disfavour than before.

'Nathan Dursley,' said Mr Sharp. 'Max was talking about him a few weeks ago. He told me that this Nathan was always taking his drink away and drinking it himself. And I told Max he ought to do something about it. That he shouldn't just let it happen! But I didn't realise he'd go this far! He's certainly taught Nathan a lesson he won't forget, hasn't he? But,' he added hastily, 'it was very very wrong of Max, and obviously he will be very severely punished.'

'Hmm,' said Mrs Grieves, tapping her desk with a pen. She turned to Max. 'I'm very disappointed in you, Max. Very disappointed indeed.'

'I'm sorry,' said Max. It seemed expected.

'Well, that's really not good enough!'

Max felt like saying: 'All right, in that case I'm *not*

sorry.' And while he was about it he might just say: 'And actually I never touched the alcohol bottles, it was Lizzie who did that, and it was never meant for anyone to drink.' But he decided to say nothing. He wasn't altogether displeased with the way things were going.

'Alcohol is very dangerous! Did you not know that?'

Max couldn't quite work out whether the expected answer to this was 'yes' or 'no'. The 'not' in the question was confusing. Mrs Grieves was waiting, so he just said, 'I'm sorry' again, though he thought it unlikely that this would be good enough this time, if it hadn't been before.

'I would be fully entitled to suspend you,' said Mrs Grieves. Max and his father both looked suitably subdued at this. Mrs Grieves tapped away with the pen a while longer, before suddenly saying: 'Max, you wait outside, while I have a word with your father.'

Max opened the door, slipped out and stood in the corridor. This development was such a surprise he didn't know what to make of it. On the whole if one person had to be sent out he was glad it had been him and not his father. But he hoped his father wasn't getting told off. He had made it sound like it was all his fault really, for putting ideas into Max's head. It was very noble and brave of him to do that, but it would be unfair if he got into trouble. Mrs Grieves couldn't suspend a parent, could she?

But five minutes later – an endless five minutes, for Max – the door opened and his father came out, giving him a secret wink.

'Come along!' he yelled. 'You are in very serious trouble, my lad!'

Max shrivelled. But then his father winked at him again, and all of a sudden Max realised that all the shouting was just for the benefit of anyone listening. He should have known, really – his father had never called him (or anybody else) 'my lad' in his entire life. It was all for show.

Mr Sharp put a firm hand on Max's shoulder and ushered him out to the car.

'Am I going home?' Max asked nervously. 'I haven't really been suspended, have I?'

'You certainly have!' roared his father. 'And you deserve it! Get in the car this minute!' He slammed the doors, revved up the engine and accelerated down the road *zooom*! like a clap of thunder.

Max was trembling. 'I've been suspended?' he whispered. He didn't feel so brave any more.

'Only for the rest of today,' said his father. 'You got off lightly. Me, now, I've got a week's detention. Hey, Max! Don't look so worried. Nobody's *really* cross with you.'

'They aren't? Then why...'

'Mrs Grieves felt that the situation required a gesture. And quite honestly, I think she was glad to get rid of us both and leave it to me to punish you. She's got two teachers to cover for, and she's got your class camped out in the hall while they fumigate your classroom. That boy must have been very, very sick. I'm ashamed of you. Thoroughly ashamed.'

'So you mean, I go back to school tomorrow?'

'That's right. And between you and me, I'd be very

surprised if anybody tries to nick anything of yours again. I think you'll find you've got a reputation, now. Take a tip from me, though – don't go swaggering around like a hero. That won't go down well with the teachers.'

'I never swagger,' said Max. 'I don't even know how.'

'I thought not,' said his father. They turned into Cleve Road and began to rattle down the lane. 'And now, I have to punish you. I promised.'

Max waited to hear the worst. Somehow he didn't think it was going to be very bad.

'You aren't allowed any alcohol for the rest of the week,' said his father.

'I suppose that's fair,' said Max. He half-thought of telling his father about the dog's urine. But maybe it wasn't worth the risk. His father might burst into laughter and shake his head with admiration at Max's creativity. But then, he might be disgusted (it was, really, disgusting) and it just wasn't worth risking that when he was in such a good mood. Dan and Lizzie knew about the dog's urine. And, more importantly, *Nathan* knew. That would have to do, for the moment. Maybe he'd tell his father the whole story some time in the future, when he was grown up. Maybe he wouldn't. He had a long time to think about it.

The rest of Max's punishment was to do boring jobs for the remainder of the day. With so many pets on the premises, boring jobs were always easy to find. Max had to clean out his hamster's cage, clean out all the guinea pigs, feed the chickens and take Bonnie for a good long walk. But apart from the first job (the hamster), which Max did on his own, it wasn't like work at all, because his father decided to take the rest of the day off and did the other things with him. And so Max had his father all to himself for three whole hours, before they had to go and fetch Dan. It had been the strangest day he could remember. It felt so very peculiar to be off school when he was perfectly well – to be pottering round with his dad while everyone else was stuck in the classroom. And then to drive *back* to school to collect his brother! How weird was that?

Dan was bursting for information. The most drastic rumours had been abounding; he had been searching for Max on and off all day, but Max had mysteriously disappeared. And now here he was, arriving in the car with their father! It was quite extraordinary.

'What's been going on?' he demanded, scrambling in and belting himself up, almost with a single movement. 'What happened? There's been all sorts of stories going round. I've heard that Nathan Dursley got taken to hospital and Mrs Allinson got drunk and was sick all over Miss Parrish, and Max was expelled!'

'My goodness,' said Mr Sharp, fascinated. 'It's like a game of Chinese Whispers. Gets passed on from one person to another until it's almost unrecognisable from the original. None of the four things you said is true. Not even one!'

'So what *did* happen? Max! Tell me!'

Max saw no reason to say anything. He had been

doing extremely well so far by leaving it to everyone else to do the talking. Leave people to themselves to try and work things out, and they seemed to come up with ideas that were much more ingenious than any Max could have managed by himself.

In any case, he hadn't quite decided what story to tell Lizzie and Dan. Probably most people didn't know that Nathan had *drunk* the potion. Everyone had arrived on the scene *after* the event. Certainly Dan hadn't managed to find this out, and you could be quite sure he had tried very hard. Max could, if he wished, simply pretend that he had cast the spell, completed the Circle of Doom (which was true!) and that the potion had worked, very very quickly and with spectacular results. Would that be best? He couldn't decide. Maybe he didn't have to, just yet. It would come to him, in time. He sat back and smiled an enigmatic smile of deep contentment.

Dan was outraged. He'd been quietly simmering in a pot of partial information all day. Everyone knew something sensational had happened, and it was fairly clear that it had happened in Miss Parrish's classroom, and there was general agreement as to the identities of the main players in the drama. One of whom was his own brother, and another the very person his brother had been due to cast a spell on that day! Which was not to say that Dan believed in magic – of course he didn't, though he was finding that he needed to remind himself of this fact more and more often. But even if you didn't believe in magic, everything he had heard sounded quite remarkable, and obviously anybody would want to know the facts. And Max wouldn't say anything! Not a word!

Dan tried to take control of the situation in the way he knew Lizzie would have done, had she been there. As soon as they arrived home he said firmly to Max: 'Let's go and feed the chickens!' This was what Lizzie always did when she wanted to get you outside for a private conversation. But:

'Dad and I did that already!' said Max, smiling sweetly.

Dan tried his father next. 'Aren't you going back upstairs to work, Dad? I'll bring you up a coffee if you like.'

'Thanks, Dan, but I rather thought I'd take the rest of the day off. I'm going to get the salad and the potatoes ready for tea. Anyone want to help me?'

'I'll help you!' said Max. 'I expect Dan's got homework to be getting on with.'

Dan frowned. 'And what are *these*?' He picked up three parcels which had been lying on top of one of the kitchen units.

Mr Sharp glanced over. 'Post for Lizzie,' he said.

'Post for Lizzie? *All* of them? But what is it?'

'How would I know? I haven't got X-ray eyes!'

Dan mooched about in darkest discontent. It seemed there was nothing he could do about the situation until Lizzie got back from drama club. Lizzie, of course, would extract all the required information out of Max in ten seconds flat.

When, at last, he heard the engine of his mother's car

approaching down Cleve Road, Dan positioned himself at the front door, ready to pull Lizzie aside and give her a lightning update.

'I'd better have a quiet word with your mother,' said Mr Sharp to Max. 'She'll have to know about you being suspended.' Max gulped. 'But don't worry about it. I'll tell her you've been thoroughly punished already.'

'Do you really need to tell her the word "suspended"? It sounds so serious.'

'You may have a point there,' said Mr Sharp. 'I'll just tell her you were sent home for the rest of the day while things were sorted out. Hey, what's this? A convoy?' A second car had appeared behind Mrs Sharp's. It was one of those big cars with an extra row of seats, called people-carriers.

Max scrambled over and peered out of the window. His mother and sister had got out of their car, and were standing in the lane looking curiously at the people-carrier.

'I don't think it's anyone we know,' said Mr Sharp. 'Must be some people come to look at The Briars, I suppose.'

'Oh good,' said Max. 'Have they got children? Can you see?'

'Bound to, with a car like that. Probably they're a big family!'

At that moment the door on the side of the people-carrier swung open, and a group of children began to climb out. First two boys of about Dan's age; then an older girl, who stopped to help a small girl jump down from the car. And finally, a large red-haired woman emerged from the driver's door, followed by a very pale and wan red-haired boy.

All of them had red hair.

It wasn't people come to look at The Briars at all. It was the entire Dursley family. An army of Dursleys arriving in force to inflict a terrible revenge on Max.

18

Take Me To Your Hamster

Mrs Sharp and Lizzie had noticed the other car following them down Cleve Road. They were just slamming their own doors shut when it turned round the last corner and drew up behind them. Lizzie gawped as a huge scrum of red-headed people tumbled out. What on earth was going on? Wasn't that *Rachel Dursley*?

A large woman, who appeared to be the only adult amongst them, emerged from the mob and strode over, one hand outstretched in greeting. The other hand was fastened firmly around the shoulder of a small red-haired boy.

'Hello!' she said to Mrs Sharp. 'Francine Dursley. You must be Max's mother.'

'Kate Sharp,' Lizzie's mother said, shaking hands in some confusion.

Max's mother, thought Lizzie. And Francine *Dursley*. And Max had gone prancing into school with a Dursley potion that very morning. She had a bad, bad feeling about this.

'I thought we ought to have a word,' said Francine Dursley. 'Sorry I had to bring all this lot with me, but their father's away all week, you know how it is.'

'Erm. Yes,' said Mrs Sharp, not knowing in the least how anything was. 'Would you – would you like to come in?' The Dursley children had formed a sort of half-circle around their mother, and were eyeing Lizzie up and down with frank curiosity.

'Just for a minute, then,' said Mrs Dursley. 'Nathan wants a word with Max. Don't you, Nathan?'

The small boy in her grip made a faint, miserable moaning noise.

The spell must have worked, Lizzie thought. And Max must have got found out. In which case, they were *all* in the most spectacular kind of trouble. Lizzie and Dan had pinched large quantities of alcohol and given them to Max to take to school. And Max had somehow screwed up. But then, what had she expected? He wasn't even eight yet. She should never have trusted him to cast a spell without supervision.

They all trooped into the house, where, in the kitchen and in varying degrees of bafflement and fear, stood Max, Dan and their father. The Dursley children (except Nathan) formed a tidy line behind their mother, and stood there waiting with a general air of pleasant anticipation, as if awaiting the raising of the curtain on a much looked-forward-to entertainment. You half expected them to start passing round drinks and popcorn.

Max's first thought had been to run and hide. But he had stayed put. He had his father right beside him, and his father was *on his side*. And his father was the biggest person present. (He had to check Mrs Dursley quite closely to be sure about this.) If the worst came to the worst and a family fight broke out, the Dursleys would outnumber the Sharps by six to five. There was no getting away from that. However, the Sharps had two grown-ups and the Dursleys had only one. And Max was certain that Lizzie was a much better fighter than that Lizzie-sized Dursley girl. And Nathan Dursley was hardly likely to be on very good form, was he? You could tell that just by looking at him. He looked like an old shirt that's just been spat out of the tumble drier. And Bonnie was sure to join in on their side. She had never bitten anybody in her life so far, but then she had never been properly provoked.

All in all, Max was confident.

Lizzie and Mrs Sharp joined the rest of their family on the far side of the table. The battle lines were drawn.

Dan was thinking: It's like the bit at the end of a detective story where the detective gathers all the suspects together and spends about ten minutes explaining how the murderer committed the incredibly ingenious crime.

Lizzie was thinking: Those Dursley children are lined up in decreasing order of height starting with Rachel, the tallest, on the left. They look exactly like the kids in *The Sound of Music*. Any minute now their father will walk in and blow a whistle and they'll all start marching and singing about their Favourite Things.

Mrs Dursley stepped forward.

'I've heard all about it,' she said.

Mr Sharp flashed a look towards his wife that said, more or less: 'This is probably not a good time for you to start asking questions. I'll explain everything later.'

Mrs Dursley tweaked Nathan's ear. 'Owww,' said Nathan, miserably.

'He told me everything. How he's been bullying your boy and taking his snacks and his drinks. The whole story came pouring out. The alcohol must have loosened his tongue. Gets that from his father, for sure. Three pints inside *him* and he'll tell you anything you want to know. Very useful, that is, as no doubt you can imagine.'

There was a long silence.

'And I told him,' continued Mrs Dursley, seeing that nobody else had anything to say, 'I told him, I won't have it! Bullying is the one thing I despise! Your boy did a fine thing to teach him such a sharp lesson. Nathan, what do you have to say to Max?'

'I'm sorry,' mumbled Nathan, eyes cast downwards.

Max felt a sudden, impish urge to say: 'Well, that's really not good enough!' But he resisted. It was almost impossible to believe that this cringing little person was the same Nathan Dursley that had blighted every day of his school life so far. He didn't even look *big* any more, without Robert Crane and Alex Matthews, and standing there next to his mother (who was admittedly enormous). And somehow, seeing the entire family lined up as if for military inspection, it was impossible not to notice that they were a good-looking bunch, in a stocky, healthy, freckled sort of way – all except for Nathan, with his piggy little watery blue eyes in that squashed, prize-fighter face.

'It's all right,' said Max. It seemed that no apology was to be demanded of him in return, even if he had done his best to poison Mrs Dursley's youngest son. Maybe she didn't like him much. You could hardly blame her.

189

There was another pause, as if nobody knew what was supposed to happen next. Then Bonnie, who had kept her distance while she assessed the nature of the invasion, nosed her way into the kitchen, followed by Lucy, the most inquisitive of the cats.

'Ohhhhh!' The smallest Dursley child, the girl standing on the far right of the row, stepped forward, picked up Lucy and cradled her in her arms.

'Don't blame anyone but yourself if you get scratched, Ruth,' said Mrs Dursley. Lucy was not a scratching sort of cat, but neither was she a cat who was always in the mood to be hugged. But on this occasion she consented to the treatment, and her body began to vibrate with long, low purrs.

Rachel and Jacob Dursley dropped to their knees and set about making a fuss of Bonnie, who licked them, adoringly, turn and turn about.

'Lovely house you've got here,' said Mrs Dursley, who apparently now considered the Nathan episode closed. 'And it's so quiet!' Snowball stalked into the room and leapt up onto a chair. 'Ohhhh!' said Ruth Dursley again. 'And all these pets!' said her mother.

'We've got chickens,' said Max.

'Chickens!' Ruth Dursley put Lucy down, went over to Max and grabbed his hand. 'Take me to see the chickens!' she commanded, in the tones of one who expects to be obeyed.

'Bossy little brat,' said Mrs Dursley, not unkindly. Max submitted meekly to being dragged out into the garden to examine the chickens. 'Makes a change for her to have someone smaller than herself to push around. Anyway, as I was saying, what a wonderful location you have here! We've been looking to move for some time but with all these bloody kids it's hard to find anything suitable. I don't suppose you're thinking of moving, are you?' she added, suddenly piercing Mr Sharp with a calculating stare.

'Erm – no, we're quite happy here actually. But the house *opposite* is for sale.'

Mr Sharp explained to his family later that he had not, at this point, been thinking very clearly. The one thing that was *crystal* clear to him was that here standing in his kitchen was a woman of indomitable will, who wanted his house. At moments like this there wasn't time to stop and think what kind of neighbour Mrs Dursley would make, let alone her flock of children and the as-yet-unseen Mr Dursley who couldn't hold his tongue when drunk. None of this crossed his mind. He was just protecting his own territory. It seemed only practical to divert attention to The Briars, across the lane, before the Dursleys marched upstairs and began deciding who would have which bedroom.

'Is it really?' Mrs Dursley went over and peered out through the kitchen window. 'I didn't notice the sign. The row these kids make in the car, it's not surprising. Let's go out and have a look. Is it the same size as this one?'

'More or less,' said Mr Sharp. 'But it's not at all modern, inside. It would need a lot doing to it, I should think.'

191

'*That's* no problem,' said Mrs Dursley. 'Give himself something useful to be getting on with at weekends instead of sitting round on his backside in front of the telly swilling lager.' She led the way out to the front to inspect The Briars, followed by the line of Dursley children and, after a few moments during which they exchanged glances expressing feelings ranging from helplessness to desperation, from perplexity to mirth, by Mr and Mrs Sharp.

Which left Dan and Lizzie. Lizzie rounded on her brother the second they were left alone.

'What happened? Did Max do the spell? What was that woman on about?'

'I don't know,' said Dan.

'You must know! You'd been home for an hour and a half before me!'

'All I know is Max got sent home for the day. And something happened to Nathan Dursley. And two of the teachers.'

'Two teachers!' Had Max been careless with his sprinkling? Unless the teachers were also called Dursley Lizzie didn't exactly understand what had happened. But all the same – two teachers! You had to be impressed.

'Where *is* he, anyway?'

'Max? He went out the back garden with that girl, ages ago.'

Lizzie and Dan raced outside. Ruth Dursley and Max were sitting on the grass by the guinea pigs' cage, the chickens presumably having been inspected and found to be satisfactory. Brandy was dozing in Ruth's lap, while Cider, who had crawled up her sleeve, suddenly poked his head out of the neck of her jumper, blinking in the daylight.

'I wish I lived here,' said Ruth Dursley. 'We could have guinea pig races. We could have guinea pig parties and teach them musical chairs. We could have talent shows and beauty competitions. We could have guinea pig Olympics. And chicken dances. We haven't got any pets at home,' she added sadly. 'There's no room.'

Lizzie cleared her throat. There seemed no possibility of getting Max on his own for a quiet word. 'Max,' she said. 'Did you do the – erm – did you do the *thing*?' It was so difficult to talk openly, with this dratted Dursley child sitting there.

But:

'Max poisoned my brother Nathan,' said Ruth Dursley, gazing at Max with open admiration.

'Don't you *like* Nathan?' Max asked her. 'I mean, he's your *brother*.'

Ruth pulled a disgusted face. 'Nobody does. My mum says he's a little sod and he's going to turn out just like his father.' This did sound just exactly like something Mrs Dursley would say.

It was not proving easy to get at the facts. 'Max.' Lizzie tried again. 'You did it? The *sprinkling*?'

'Of course I did,' said Max, catching hold of Cider, who had climbed down Ruth's back and was making a bid for freedom.

Lizzie heaved a deep sigh of contentment. She would

extract the details later; she had found out the most important fact. The spell had been cast, and it had worked. It appeared to have worked with much greater and more immediate effect than any previous spell. All the evidence was that her powers were growing stronger by the day. Perhaps before long her spells would take *instant* effect, which would be profoundly satisfying, especially as her wishes had stubbornly stopped coming true. Clearly she needed to work on her technique in that area. But she was only thirteen. She had *plenty* of time.

'Have you got any more pets?' Ruth was asking Max.

'There's the budgies,' said Max. 'And another cat you haven't seen. And my hamster Zippy. He's in my bedroom.'

Ruth scrambled to her feet and put Brandy back in the hutch. 'Take me to your hamster!' she ordered, sounding very much like an alien newly-landed on earth who hadn't been paying full attention during English vocabulary lessons.

All four of them trailed back into the kitchen, to find the other Dursleys returned from outside, and Mrs Dursley talking on her mobile. She gestured frantically at her younger daughter, covered the mouthpiece with one hand and bellowed, 'Ruth! Don't you *dare* disappear again!' before resuming her conversation. 'So we'll see you in twenty minutes then? Wonderful! Goodbye for the moment then, Louise.' She clicked the phone off and stowed it away in her bag.

'How about that then?' she crowed. 'Louise from the estate agent's will be over directly to show us round the house. Sounds as if they're finding it difficult to shift. How long did you say it had been on the market?'

'A couple of months,' said Mrs Sharp, faintly.

'I know Louise,' Max said, surprisingly. 'She waved at me.'

Waved at you? thought Lizzie. And when was *this*?

'Tell you what,' said Mr Sharp. 'If you're going to be waiting, why don't we all have a drink and some crisps? Kate . . . ' – he turned to his wife – '. . . why don't you pop upstairs and change into something cooler, and when you come back down there'll be a nicely chilled glass of Chardonnay waiting for you.'

'If you don't mind, I think I will,' said Mrs Sharp, who usually changed and had a shower as soon as she got in from work, and was starting to look distinctly frayed at the edges. Her husband opened the fridge. 'Glass of Chardonnay, Mrs – erm – Dursley?'

'Francine,' said Mrs Dursley. 'God, yes, I wouldn't mind. I'm surprised you've got any alcohol left, actually. Thought my son had swallowed most of it.'

Mr Sharp gulped, and busied himself with distributing cans of Coke and Fanta to all the children. Except Nathan, who was not prepared to trust any drinks provided by members of the Sharp family, and who in any case felt that anything fizzy might cause his stomach, which was at present simmering very gently, to start bubbling and seething and boiling all over again.

Mrs Dursley sipped her wine with satisfaction. 'Thank you very much, Mr . . . ?'

'Jim.'

'And where did you get to, madam?' Mrs Dursley's attention snapped away in the direction of Ruth.

'Went out the garden to look at the chickens. And the guinea pigs.'

'Guinea pigs as well?'

'Four of them,' said Ruth. 'Brandy, Cider, Whisky and Rum.' Her mother snorted loudly as if to say, well, *there's* a surprise.

Mr Sharp tore open a few family-size crisp packets and tipped all the crisps into a large bowl. 'Oh, don't go to any bother,' said Mrs Dursley, and 'It's no bother at all,' said Mr Sharp. Everyone present knew that these were just meaningless noises that grown-ups made. For a few minutes there was silence, broken only by the sound of munching.

A car drew up outside, making a grand total of *four* cars parked at the end of Cleve Road. This was probably the all-time record, except for parties. 'That must be Louise now,' said Mrs Dursley, rising to her feet. 'Come along, all you lot. You've been under everyone's feet here quite long enough. Where's Ruth gone *now*?'

'Went upstairs with my brother to see the hamster,' said Dan.

Mrs Dursley sighed. 'Send her over if you see her,' she said, and swept out of the room, taking her wine glass and four remaining children with her.

Lizzie went over to the window and had a good look.

'So that's Louise, is it?' She nodded towards the smartly dressed blonde woman who was just escorting Mrs Dursley and the junior Dursleys up the path towards the front door of The Briars.

'That's what?' Dan was only half paying attention.

'Louise. That woman. Max said he knows her. Said she waved at him! When did that happen, I wonder?'

Dan felt a sudden urgent need to change the subject.

'Look,' he said hastily. 'Post! For you!' What with all the bizarre happenings of the past hour, Lizzie's parcels had been forgotten.

'*All* for me?' Never had a change of subject been more effective. *Three* parcels all addressed to Lizzie! Apart from Christmas and birthdays, you could go the entire year without getting a single parcel, usually.

She tore open the smallest of the parcels, pulled out a letter and read:

'Many thanks for your entry in our recent Dr Who contest. We are delighted to inform you that you have won a runners-up prize of a unique limited issue Tardis pencil sharpener!'

Lizzie shook the parcel and out fell the pencil sharpener. It was about three inches tall. It looked like a little blue phone box. It had a pencil-sized hole in the bottom. It was – a Tardis pencil sharpener.

'Well done!' said Dan. 'All you need now is a pencil and you're laughing!'

Wordlessly, Lizzie ripped the second parcel open.

'Congratulations!' she read. 'You are one of the lucky prizewinners in the *Satellite TV Weekly* Star Wars Contest (in association with Sony Playstation)! We have great pleasure in enclosing your runners-up prize of a special limited edition Darth Maul dual shock analogue control Playstation 2 controller, with state-of-the-art feedback technology!'

Dan was laughing so much he had to sit down.

'Brilliant!' he said. 'All you need now is a Playstation 2 and you're away!'

Lizzie's hand paused over the third parcel.

'Go on,' said Dan. 'You know you want to.'

Lizzie shrugged, and opened the final parcel.

'Dear *Go Girl!* Prizewinner!' she read. 'Blah blah blah blah blah, runners-up prize of a fabulous video...' She shook the package, and out fell a video of *Sabrina the Teenage Witch*.

Dan managed to catch his breath for long enough to point out how incredibly appropriate this would be for Lizzie, if only she had a video recorder.

Lizzie clenched her fists. So what if it hadn't gone quite as planned? She would just keep on entering competitions (and wishing) until she got the things that went with these things. She had made an excellent start.

Across the road, the Dursley party had emerged from The Briars and were touring the garden, while the woman Louise looked on approvingly.

'Wait here,' said Lizzie, sharply. She went and stood outside the front door. The woman Louise, standing waiting by the front gate of The Briars, gave her a friendly wave.

It was all the encouragement Lizzie needed.

'Hi there,' she said, crossing over the road.

'Hello!' Louise had gleaming white teeth in a wide smile whch seemed almost engraved onto her face. It was the kind of expression generally confined to people who work in professions that require people to buy things.

Lizzie beamed back.

'So,' she said, trying to sound more confident than she really felt inside – 'what happened to those other people you showed round? Didn't they like it in the end?'

'I'm afraid not. Such a shame, that was. But Mrs Clarkson didn't like the kitchen at all. And of course, it didn't really help, her being taken so poorly like that ... hello, Mrs Dursley! Would you like another look inside the house?'

Lizzie looked round at Dan, who was watching from the kitchen window, his face scrumpled up in horror. *Yes*! she mouthed, and punched the air. *Yes yes yes*! Nobody, but nobody, could keep anything secret from Lizzie Sharp for long. Dan had been dead cunning. All due credit to him for that. But she would always, always triumph in the end.

The Dursleys departed in the Dursleymobile ten minutes later. It was quite a struggle to get Ruth to leave; she had attached herself like a limpet to Max, whom she seemed to regard as something of a superhero. 'You'll see him again on Saturday,' said her mother, heaving the wriggling girl into the back seat and snapping the seatbelt shut *click*. 'We're coming back with your father to show him round the house. Saturday afternoons are always the best time. He's so mad to get back for the sport he'll say yes to anything. Hope to see you all then!' She climbed into the driver's seat, executed a three-point turn and drove off, with a wave over her shoulder and a flurry of toots on the horn.

'Did I just dream all that?' asked Mrs Sharp.

'I think you must have done,' said her husband. 'You'll wake up in five minutes and tell me all about it. I'll probably have to fetch you coffee in bed while you recover.'

Max tugged his father's arm. 'Dad. Are the Dursleys going to move into The Briars?'

'They will if Mrs Dursley's got anything to do with it,' his father said wryly.

Max knew what he meant. And, all of a sudden, it seemed that all the spells and the magic had simply brought them right back to where they started. They'd got rid of the Potwards surely enough, but now look what was happening! They'd come full circle. Circle of Doom, he thought, in amazement. Could anything be more doomed than life with Nathan Dursley as a neighbour? He had never really understood the importance of sprinkling the potions to the North, the South, the East and the West, but he knew a real live Circle of Doom when he saw one. He was *in* one!

'Don't look so glum, Max,' Mr Sharp said kindly. 'You wanted a family with lots of children to move in. It's just exactly what you were hoping for!'

'Not if one of them was going to be Nathan Dursley!'

'Oh, I don't think you've got much to worry about there,' said his father. 'I don't think I've ever seen a little boy look so thoroughly crushed.'

Max had to agree with that. And even as he thought about it, Nathan somehow seemed to *shrink*, from a great hulking prize fighter to an ordinary snivelly little boy. If the Dursleys did come to live opposite, the Nathan who moved in wouldn't be the strutting Nathan he knew from school. It would be the *home* Nathan, who seemed by and large to be considered by the rest of his family to be fairly useless. And Max had lived here his whole life. It was his own territory. And he'd have that Ruth on his side for sure. In fact if today was anything to go by, she'd never *leave* his side. And really, guinea pig Olympics and chicken dances sounded the best fun in the world.

And of course, if Nathan did step out of line, Max would teach him a very sharp lesson indeed. He still had that second bottle of Dursley potion, buried in its secret hiding place under the hedge. And he wouldn't hesitate to use it.

'Now,' said Mrs Sharp. 'Will somebody please tell me what's been going on? What had Max done to that child? Why did he look so ill? And where did the *alcohol* come into it?'

'Oh dear,' said Mr Sharp. 'Let's go inside, and we'll tell you the whole gruesome story, over tea. Anyone fancy a pizza?'